Also by Kirk Scroggs

Tales of a Sixth-Grade Muppet

Tales of a Sixth-Grade Muppet: Clash of the Class Clowns

The Wiley & Grampa Creature Features series

Tales of a SIXTH-GRADE MUPPET

THE GOOD, THE BAD, AND THE FUZZY

Story and Art by **KIRK SCROGGS**

Little, Brown and Company

Hachette Book Group
237 Park Avenue, New York, NY 10017
Visit our website at www.lb-kids.com

Little, Brown and Company is a division of Hachette Book Group, Inc. The Little, Brown name and logo are trademarks of Hachette Book Group, Inc.

The publisher is not responsible for websites (or their content) that are not owned by the publisher.

First Edition: September 2012

ISBN 978-0-316-18312-3

10 9 8 7 6 5 4 3 2 1

RRD-C

Printed in the United States of America

Book design by Maria Mercado

To Nils and Finn

Special thanks to

Steve Deline; Joanna Stamfel-Volpe; Jim Lewis and his band
of merry Muppets; Andrea Spooner; Danielle Barthel; Diane, Corey,
Charlotte, and Candace Scroggs; Harold Aulds; Camilla
and Marisa Deline; Mark Mayes; Alejandra Arellano; Joe Kocian;
and the Disney crew.

And a special boomerang salmon salute to Erin Stein, Maria Mercado,
JoAnna Kremer, David Caplan, Jessica Bromberg, Erin McMahon,
and the Little, Brown crew. Yaaaaaay!

Since We Last Spoke

by Danvers Blickensderfer

Life has been a real whirlwind since I transformed into a Muppet, let me tell you! Ever since that bright flash of green at 12:22 AM, I've barely had time to write and brilliantly illustrate these updates, what with being The Great Gonzo's personal assistant, Dr. Honeydew's personal ~~guinea pig~~ scientific subject, and a tween idol. Not to mention all the good work I do for the community.

CHARITY WORK

Local cleanup Efforts

Lecturing on the Evils of fame

I even had my own reality-TV series, which did so well that I got a personal call from the head of Bwavo Channel.

Okay, so we got canceled. To be honest, I've been trying to focus on getting back to my old self, anyway.

My Muppetmorphosis seems to have affected more than just yours truly. The worlds of fact and fiction, fantasy and reality, savory and sweet are getting dangerously mixed up.

I mean, why would the Muppet Theater pop up in boring ol' Block City, when everyone knows it should be in Hollywood?

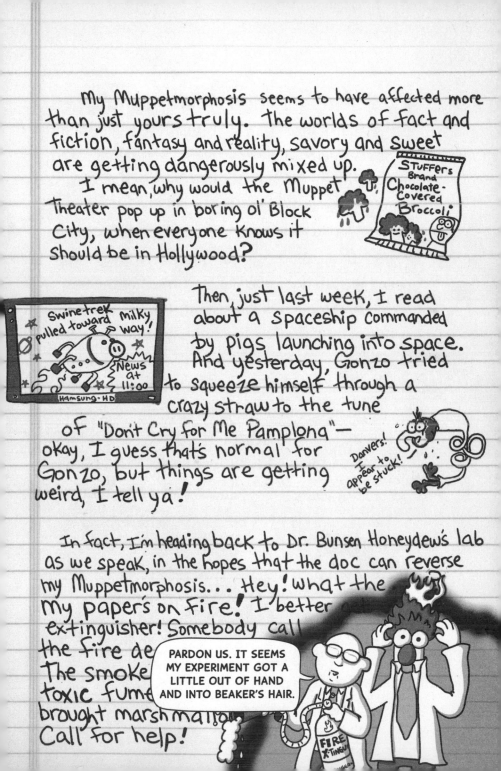

STUFFERS
Brand
Chocolate-
Covered
Broccoli

Then, just last week, I read about a spaceship commanded by pigs launching into space. And yesterday, Gonzo tried to squeeze himself through a crazy straw to the tune of "Don't Cry for Me Pamplona"—okay, I guess that's normal for Gonzo, but things are getting weird, I tell ya!

Swine-trek pulled toward milky way!
News at 11:00
Hamsung-HD

Danvers! I appear to be stuck!

In fact, I'm heading back to Dr. Bunsen Honeydew's lab as we speak, in the hopes that the doc can reverse my Muppetmorphosis... Hey! what the my paper's on fire! I better extinguisher! Somebody call the fire de The smoke toxic fume brought marshmallow Call for help!

PARDON US. IT SEEMS MY EXPERIMENT GOT A LITTLE OUT OF HAND AND INTO BEAKER'S HAIR.

FIRE X-Tingui

When Dr. Honeydew requested that I meet him at his lab at Eagle Talon Academy, for some weird reason he asked me to bring my dad. I also had my pet rat, Curtis, at my side, as well as Pasquale, my best friend and safety officer—which was a good move, because when we arrived, the place was an inferno! As soon as we opened the lab door, the pungent smell of the burnt hair of Dr. Honeydew's assistant, Beaker, filled the air. (It smells kinda like charred tangerine peels and teddy-bear stuffing, in case you were wondering.) Flames were quickly spreading across the room. Luckily, Pasquale had his own personal X-3750 Fire Extinguisher with him, and he blasted the fire with foam. My dad helped fight the flames as well.

My dad dousing the fire with flammable powder actually worked out nicely—the wind from the explosion extinguished the flames. Of course, I'd guess it also did about a hundred thousand dollars worth of damage. Oh, well…it's all in the name of science.

"Whoooweeee!" I said, wiping my forehead. "That was a scorcher! I'm honored, Doc! All this destruction just from trying to reverse my transformation."

Dr. Honeydew shook his head. "Actually, we were trying to make hot fudge using cocoa atoms, nitroglycerin, lavender-scented hand lotion, and a propane torch." He pulled out his notepad and scribbled, "Note to self: Next time, use less hand lotion."

Pasquale leaned over to me and whispered, "Surely he didn't call us over here to watch him make explosive fudge."

"Astute observation, young man," said Dr. Honeydew, walking us over to the corner of his lab that wasn't a pile of burning embers. "What I wanted to show you before we got distracted was this."

Dr. Honeydew approached a large round object with a dusty sheet draped over it. With one dramatic swoop he ripped off the sheet to unveil…

"Whoooaaaaa!" I whoa'd. In front of us was a metallic podlike contraption. It was as tall as our refrigerator and looked kinda like a giant Easter egg crossed with a cyborg. It had one door on the front and a big cable poking out the back, which stretched across the room and attached to an identical pod.

"That's some set of telephone booths you got there, Doc," said my dad.

Dr. Honeydew flipped a switch and the pods lit up with blinking lights, and steam billowed out of the pod doors. "These aren't telephone booths, my friend. Danvers, I want you to step into the first unit. Then, Mr. Blickensderfer, you will step inside with your son. If my calculations are correct, with the flip of this switch here, you both will be exploded into atoms, then reconfigured and transported to that pod over there. Danvers, I believe the extra Blickensderfer DNA from your dad will force out any residual Muppetness."

My dad gave me a look. "I thought you brought me over here to watch the Patriarchs game on the doctor's big-screen TV?"

"Tell me about it," grumbled Pasquale. "He told me we were just gonna hang out together tonight, no science experiments, no Gonzo stunts, and definitely no Transportaters."

"Come on!" I said. "We spent, like, an hour together today already."

"Running up the bleachers in gym class with

Coach Kraft shooting ice water at us from a Silly-Squirter doesn't count," said Pasquale.

I tried to comfort Pasquale. "I know you get a little frustrated, but I just gotta find out why this happened to me, and how to go back to my old self. Don't get me wrong—it's great being a Muppet and all, but it's not always a picnic."

The drawbacks of Being a Muppet
by Danvers Blickensderfer

Felty skin is a magnet for thistles and stickers (and don't get me started on Velcro!).

Velcro darts

Flip-top mouth is really annoying on roller coasters.

Philly's Hot Link

Superabsorbent body can make showering heavy going.

Uncontrollable puns come out at inappropriate moments.

Look at the bright side, Miss Piggy. You always said you wanted to work with a big **cast!** This could be your lucky **break!**

Hmph! (karate chop brewing.

"Son," said my dad, "I know you are hankering to get back to your old self, but I'm not sure having your atoms recombobulated—"

"That's not a real word, but I like it," interrupted Pasquale.

"I'm just not sure this is the safest plan," my dad finished.

"Oh, don't worry. It's perfectly safe," Dr. Honeydew assured us. "There *is* a forty-five-percent chance that you might vanish into the atmosphere during transport, but that's neither here nor there. And there's a remote possibility you and your son could be combined into one being. A molecular mash-up, if you will."

ME AND HIM, COMBINED INTO ONE BEING? I CAN'T GO TO SCHOOL WITH THAT MUSTACHE!

"Perhaps we should do what scientists conducting dangerous experiments have been doing for centuries: Test them out on their assistants first," Dr. Honeydew suggested.

"Meep?" squeaked Beaker.

The steel pod rumbled like an idling jet engine as Beaker stepped in, shivering and meeping feverishly.

"Don't be concerned about bodily harm, Beaker," Dr. Honeydew comforted his assistant. "We will all be behind a protective safety barrier over ten feet away when you are vaporized."

"Maybe you should wrap him in foil, Doc," advised my dad. "It'll seal in juices and lock in freshness."

After Beaker was secured in his pod, Dr. Honeydew hit various switches and levers on a huge computer command console in the middle of the room.

At the end of his countdown, the doc threw a big green lever and the room began to rumble. Blue lightning crackled around the pod and a bright white flash and an explosive sonic boom left us dazed and confused. Curtis cowered on my shoulder.

When the dust settled, Dr. Honeydew turned to us and said, "If the test was successful, Beaker should have been transported through time and space to the far pod."

Suddenly, the door on the second pod flew off its hinges and Beaker stepped out of the smoky mist with a *klang*! That's right, a *klang*! Beaker had been transformed into a steel, half-human, half-robot being. His skin was shiny metallic, his eyes were glowing orbs, his hair was like wiry steel cables, and his hands were coated in a nonstick Tufflon coating, perfect for frying eggs and dishwasher safe.

"What's up with Beaker?" I asked. "He looks like

my mom's combination toaster,
food processor, coffeemaker, and
bunion massager."

MEEP!

"Oh, dear," said Dr. Honeydew,
rushing to his computer to review
his files. "I must examine the data
to uncover what went wrong."
He clacked away on the keyboard,
looking for answers. Then Curtis scurried up, pointed
to the screen, and squeaked.

"Oh, my!" shouted Dr. Honeydew. "You're onto
something there, my furry little helper. It's exactly as
I had feared!"

"What is it, Doc?" I said.

"Your laboratory rat just pointed out that I was storing a box of old kitchen appliances in the other pod. I had totally forgotten about them and now I'm afraid that Beaker has been fused with the best kitchen technology of the nineteen seventies!"

Dramatic music filled the room as Beaker opened his mouth with a rusty creak and coughed up a piece of half-burnt toast, which landed at my feet.

"Doc, I think I've decided to wait until your Transportater has had a few more test runs before I let you reconfigure my atoms," said my dad.

I had to agree. "Yeah, sorry, Dr. Honeydew. As much as I'd love to be able to produce my own strawberry

Toaster Tarts, I don't think I can handle any more bizarre transformations this year."

Suddenly there was a loud knock at the door, and the principal of Eagle Talon Academy, Sam Eagle, flung it open.

"It was nothing, Mr. Eagle," I assured him.

"Oh, hello, young Blickensderfer," Sam continued. "Have you given any more thought to our discussion on enrollment?"

I totally did not want Pasquale to hear this right now. "Uh...not yet, sir," I squeaked as Pasquale gave me a seriously dirty look.

"Well, don't think about it for too long," huffed Sam. "Numerous students have sacrificed a lot to enroll in this establishment...mostly their dignity. Oh, and, Beaker, your new look is electrifying. Very utilitarian."

As soon as Sam left, I could feel Pasquale's icy stare burning a hole through me. "What?!" I shrugged.

"What did he mean 'our discussion on enrollment'?" Pasquale snapped. "You're thinking of leaving Coldrain Middle School, aren't you? You're thinking of leaving me!"

"Maybe I've thought about it...just a little bit." I squirmed. "Just about the school, I mean. It *is* the only school that specializes in helping students achieve their full artistic potential."

WOULD ANYONE LIKE AN ICE-CREAM CONE?

I could tell Pasquale was pretty upset. I had discussed the possibility of going to Eagle Talon with my folks, and they were kind of okay with it, sort of, but I hadn't even breathed a word of it to Pasquale. He might seem shy and quiet on the outside, but deep down, he's a volcano of raw emotion just waiting to erupt. Well, okay, maybe he's more like one of those volcanoes you make for science projects out of baking soda and vinegar, but he could still erupt.

"Look, Pasquale," I said, trying to comfort him. "Let's not worry about it right now. I haven't even made up my mind. We need to focus on getting me back to my old self."

But Pasquale just walked off, his shoulders slumped.

Dr. Honeydew moseyed up beside me. "Danvers. About getting you back to your old self—we should talk about that."

This didn't sound promising.

"I'm afraid that there is a distinct possibility that your Muppetmorphosis could be a permanent condition. I'm not ready to give up hope just yet, but

I'm darn close....Being a Muppet forever is a reality you must be willing to consider."

"Permanent condition? Be a Muppet forever?" I sighed, plopping down on a crate full of preserved planarian worms. "That's heavy."

"Actually, quite light," said Dr. Honeydew. "The average Muppet weighs only four point three pounds."

My dad pulled up a box of mutated fungus spores and sat next to me. "Son, let me tell you a little story...."

Whenever my dad says, "Let me tell you a little story," my brain fills up with images of The Great Gonzo juggling Alaskan salmon on top of the Statue of Liberty. I think it's a defense mechanism to keep me from being bored to death, like when a lizard lets its own tail fall off so it doesn't get caught by a predator. I usually catch the end of his stories, though, so at least I can get the gist of them.

Dad clamped a hand on my shoulder and said, "I guess what I'm trying to say, son, is that maybe you were meant to be what you were meant to be."

Easier said than felt.

After a stressful night of tossing and turning with thoughts of forever being orange and fuzzy and of Pasquale hating me for deserting him, I actually woke up in pretty good spirits.

When I arrived at school, I saw Pasquale at his locker. From the look on his face, I thought he either had just smelled a rotten egg or was in a seriously bad mood. I was sure he was still worried that I was leaving Coldrain. Somehow, I had to get him to not be miffed at me. We were leaving for spring break in just a few days, and there was no way I wanted to spend my vacation with bad blood in the air. In fact, as a general rule, I'd rather there not be *any* blood in the air.

I decided to use my patented Rapid-Fire Pun Attack, a full-on assault of bad jokes that would chip away at Pasquale's surly exterior until he couldn't help but give in to my charms.

"Hey, Pasquale!" I said, all peppy-like. "Look, dude, I should apologize for last night. I know I made you feel like a watch that's stopped running."

Pasquale gave me a cold look, with one eyebrow raised, and said, "How so?"

"You were *ticked* off! Get it? Ticked, as in tick-tock?"

But Pasquale wasn't having it. "I know what you're trying to do. You think you can make me forget I'm angry with you with a bunch of bad puns. It's so predictable. Now you'll make a million ticking-clock jokes, trying to get me to giggle. Well, it's not going to work."

A Blickensderfer never turns down a challenge!

"Oooh! I've had it!" Pasquale bellowed, slamming his locker with enough force to rattle little Timmy Bender's braces. Pasquale barged off down the hall.

I couldn't believe it. Pasquale must have really been mad to resist my time-tested wit. I could usually break him with just four puns and a knock-knock joke.

"Where are you going?" I called out.

"To see the school nurse!" barked Pasquale. "I'm suddenly feeling nauseous."

"Don't worry!" I said as he marched away in a huff. "I don't even think I'm going to go to Eagle Talon! There's, like, a ninety-percent chance I'm staying right here at Coldrain!" Which was true, give or take fifty percent.

SEEMED LIKE THOSE BAD CLOCK JOKES WENT ON FOREVER.

YOU KNOW WHAT THEY SAY: "TIME FLIES WHEN YOU'RE HAVING *PUNS*"! HO! HO! HO!

Suddenly, Kip, formerly known as "the good friend who kicked me out of his obnoxious boy band and became my mortal enemy before chillaxing and becoming my friend again," came running up to me. His normally perfect hair looked frazzled, and his eyes were quivering with stress—well, I actually couldn't see his eyes through his ridiculous bangs, but I'm sure they were quivering. His bandmates Danny and Cody were with him, and they looked just as distraught.

"Dude, I need your advice, yo," he whimpered.

"I don't know if I'm in any condition to give advice," I said. "I just drove away my best friend in the world."

"This is about something much more important than your friendship with Pasquale!" cried Kip.

I said, "Like what?"

"Me, yo!"

Kip started really freaking out and babbling incoherently—something about nursery rhymes and Little Bo Peep.

SNAP OUT OF IT, MAN!

WHAP!

25

Kip finally came to his senses. "Whoa! I can't believe you just slapped me. Good thing you're made of felt, or that could have hurt."

"I promise you, I took almost no pleasure in doing it. Now, what in the world has you so upset?"

"It's my career, dude! My reputation! My dignity! They're all about to take a belly flop in the cesspool of shame, yo!"

I rolled my eyes. "Quit being so dramatic and just tell me what's wrong!"

Kip held a CD up to my face and said, "This is what's wrong!"

"*Tea Party in the Garden*, Yo, with Emo Shun?" I said, trying to hold back a giggle. "Boy! That is wrong! When did you do this?"

"We just recorded it last week," Kip cried. "We're supposed to release it on the Internet at five PM, but now I'm starting to have second thoughts, yo!"

"I'm surprised you ever had first thoughts," I said with a laugh. "What made you guys want to record an album for little kids?"

L'HUMILIATION!

THIS CD'S NICK NACK PADDY WHACK, YO!

"Dude, I panicked," said Kip. "Emo Shun's popularity has been on the skids lately. We needed to do something bold."

"But music for toddlers?" I said. "How's that gonna help your rep?"

"Someone told us that the kiddie market is where it's at, man! But now I'm not so sure. This could be more embarrassing than the time I sang 'La Cucaracha' in a green leotard."

Suddenly, I got suspicious. "Who told you this would be a good idea?"

Kip looked around nervously. "It was…it was your little sister, dude."

My flip-top mouth opened so wide I could see the backs of my shoes. "My sister! You took advice from my sister?"

"I figured she knew all about what's popular with kids, yo. Look at all her Fluffleberries success!"

"My sister would advise a baby mouse to take tango lessons from a boa constrictor just for her own enjoyment!" I ranted. "You have to stop this from being released immediately!"

"I know! I know!" said Kip. "But I feel kinda lousy. Your sis was so excited about it. I bet she's anxiously awaiting the album to drop as we speak."

I had to laugh. "I think I have a pretty good idea what Chloe's doing right now."

Kip was beside himself. "What am I gonna do, dude? My cool card will get revoked for sure if this gets out!"

Suddenly, Scrant and Greevus walked by, shouting out to us, "Dude! Love that poison ivy song! Itchy itchy itchy, yo! Scratchy scratchy scratchy, yo!"

GIRL, DON'T BE RASH! GIRL, DON'T BE CRUEL!

Then some girls skipping down the hall stopped and called out, "Hi, Danvers! Hi, Kip! Awesome new track!" They shuffled off, giggling and looking back at us.

"Dude, what's going on?" asked Kip.

I leaned in and said, "They're singing our poison ivy song."

"I thought that tune was ancient history, yo."

In case you haven't been keeping up, Kip's band, Emo Shun, and my band, Mon Swoon, joined forces a few months back to form Mon Emo Shun Swoon, or M.E.S.S. for short. We recorded only one track: "Girl, Don't Be Rash." We thought the song was gonna be a huge hit, but due to a mix-up when Pasquale posted it online, when kids listened to it…well, you know that magazine article in *Moral Outrage Weekly* that claimed rock music turns kids into little monsters? Let's just say listening to our download turned kids into monsters, for real! Zombies, to be precise.

Button Hauser walked up to me and Kip looking all dewy-eyed.

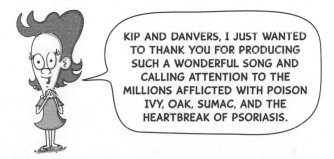

Then, more and more kids approached us, raving about that silly song.

"How is everybody hearing a song that turned the student body into zombies, got us in hot water, and has been buried for months?" asked Kip.

"I figured no one in their right mind would ever wanna hear that track again," I added.

AGAIN? I NEVER WANTED TO HEAR IT THE FIRST TIME! HO! HO! HO!

That's when Kip's cell phone rang. "'Sup, yo?" he answered.

HOLA! I HAVE THE EXCITING NEWS, OKAY!

Kip turned to us and announced, "Hey! Pepe's got some good news for us, yo! I'm gonna put him on speakerphone."

NO NEED FOR THAT, OKAY. I'M RIGHT UP HERE. I SNUCK THROUGH THE AIR-CONDITIONED VENTS LIKE THE NINJA, OKAY.

"Wow, Pepe!" I said. "You must have something really important to say to sneak in and tell us in person."

"First of all, everything Pepe the King Prawn says is important, okay. Second, I come here to tell you that, as your talented agent, I licensed your very catchy skin-problem song 'Girl, Don't Be Rash' to be used in a commercial for Ivy League Poison Ivy Itch Crème, okay. It aired last night during the Porcelain Bowl football game."

"Poison Ivy Itch Crème?" I said.

SÍ, MY FRIEND. POISON IVY CRÈME IS HUGE THIS YEAR. IT IS ALL OVER THE TUBE AND SPREADING ACROSS THE NATION.

"That's why everyone's been talking about the song, dude," Kip said, smiling. "They must have seen that commercial."

Pepe started to crawl back up into the air vent, saying, "I'm telling you, this M.E.S.S. is going to be huuuuuge, okay! Now, if you will excuse me, I have to go break the good news to Gonzo, Scooter, Fozzie, and the scary one with the drumsticks, okay. *Adios!*"

Pepe took off, back up into the ventilation shaft. I turned to Kip. "Well, it looks like your prayers have been answered. You won't need to release your Little Bo Peep record after all."

"*C'est un miracle!*" praised Danny.

Kip frowned and said, "Yeah, but what do I do with the five hundred CDs I printed?"

"I say hire my sister to glitterize them and sell them as coasters. And hey, stop worrying. We've got a new hit song on our hands. Things are looking up."

All of a sudden, a dark shadow fell over us and things were definitely looking up. Actually, it was me that was looking—up the hairy, flared nostrils of my greatest nightmare.

It was Beebus Spracklin, my former arch-nemesis. Two years earlier, he had been the Incredible Hulk of our elementary school, stomping through the hallways and sending the other kids stampeding away in all directions. Beebus was the size of an industrial fridge, with about half the brainpower. I was pretty sure he'd been shaving since the first grade, and he always had a thick layer of motor oil and mustard under his fingernails. He had left a year ago, apparently to attend a big angry gorilla training academy. I was terrified to see he was back, and about four feet taller.

"Uh...hey, Beebus." Kip gulped. "Long time no see. We've, uh...really noticed your absence, yo."

"Aw, thanks! It's great to see you again." Beebus snorted before ripping Kip's new CD out of his hands. "What's this?"

Beebus held up the CD and cackled, "*Tea Party in the Garden, Yo,* with Emo Shun? Ha! How cute!"

Kip chuckled nervously, "Oh, that? That's just a practical joke, dude. A goof."

"Oh, don't be modest." Beebus laughed. "You're selling yourself short. I'm gonna make sure everyone gets to hear this little beauty!" He stuck the CD in his pocket.

"I just remembered, I gotta be going," said Kip, shuffling away. "I have to press and steam my hoodie before Mr. Piffle's class. See ya!"

"*Au revoir!*" added Danny as he darted off with Kip and Cody, leaving me to face this angry rhino by my lonesome.

Beebus gave me an evil grin. "And then there's Danvers! How I've missed our time together. I heard you had turned into a Muppet, but I didn't believe it until now. This is gonna make my life a whole lot easier!"

"How's that?" I asked.

"Now that you're a lot lighter, it won't strain my back when I dangle you over the john for a swirlie!" He picked me up by my ankle and carted me off down the hall.

As the big galoot dunked me over and over in the boys'-room toilet, my head swirled with wonderful memories of my times with Beebus past.

thanks For The Memories, Beebus
by Danvers Blickensderfer

Our First Conversation

Hey, stunt boy! Did I give you permission to drink outta my water fountain?

Fourth-Grade Show-and-tell

Look! Danvers is wearing bunny boxers!

Ha! Ha! Ha!

Fashion advice

I must say the spaghetti is the perfect accessory to your ensemble.

Looking out for one another

I cannot tell a lie... he did it!

Bonding in the fifth grade

Ha Ha! I glued your hand to the school bus!

COLDRAIN MIDDLE
EL AUTO BUS

38

After school I really wanted to get the return of Beebus off my mind, not to mention get the nasty toilet water out of my hair. On top of that, I couldn't stop thinking about what my dad had said to me the night before: "Maybe you were meant to be what you were meant to be." Was I really meant to be a Muppet? And was I transformed for a reason? There had to be an answer out there somewhere. But for now, I really needed to relax.

And what better way to relax than to assist The Great Gonzo with a death-assuring—er, death-*defying* stunt involving airborne projectiles? I headed to the Muppet Theater for my internship with Gonzo.

DANVERS! GREAT NEWS! THE MUSEUM OF ABNORMAL ART WANTS TO INDUCT ME INTO THEIR HALL OF FAME, SO I'VE COME UP WITH A STUNT THAT WILL BLOW THEIR SOCKS OFF! RIZZO, PREPARE THE LAUNCHER!

"Aye, aye, Cap'n!" Rizzo replied, saluting as he ran backstage.

The sound of this had even me a little worried. "Launcher? What kind of stunt is this?"

Gonzo whipped out a diagram and spread it out on the table in front of me. "I'm glad you asked! Imagine me going one-on-one in a game of badminton with a high-powered cannon in the greatest match since King George the Brawny challenged Venus Wiggums at the Button-Fly Open in 1824. And guess what we'll be using instead of a badminton birdie?"

"Uh…a real birdie?" I said.

"I actually thought of that, but Camilla quickly vetoed the idea with a sharp peck to my shin!" Gonzo ran up to a big red curtain and pulled it back to reveal a giant piano. "No, sir! I will be playing badminton using an actual seven-hundred-pound grand piano launched from twenty yards!"

"Are you crazy?" I said. "You can't face an airborne grand piano with a dinky badminton racket!"

"You're right! Rizzo, better make it a baby grand piano!"

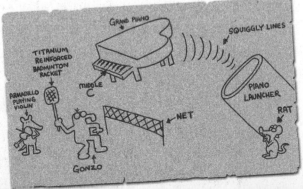

"I already advised him that this stunt is suicide," came a voice from behind me. It was Pasquale. I was so happy to see him, but he still looked a little irritable.

"Look, Pasquale," I said. "I'm sorry I was so obnox—"

Pasquale put one hand out to silence me. "Don't speak. I won't stay mad for long. I just need a little time to calm down, dude."

"But I told you I'm not even sure I'm leaving yet—"

"Actually, I got a surprise dunk from a dark figure from our past," I said.

"Vlad the Impaler?" cried Gonzo.

"Uh…no. Just someone who used to terrorize me and Pasquale back in the day."

Pasquale suddenly looked like he had seen a ghost wielding a flamethrower. "You mean…*him?*"

I nodded. "Yes, *him.*"

Pasquale swayed like he was going to pass out. "Dude, now there's no way you can leave me at Coldrain, not with *him* lurking the hallways!"

"What's with all the emphasis on the 'hims'?" came a gruff but glamorous voice from behind me. It was Miss Piggy. She was with Kermit and her assistant, Hockney, who each carried about twenty boxes and bags from one of Piggy's wild, uncontrolled shopping sprees. "Kermie dear, just set my purchases over there so Hockney can research them online before he places them in my wardrobe."

"Research them online?" Kermit grunted, buckling under the weight of the shopping bounty.

BUT OF COURSE. *MOI* MUST BE CERTAIN HER PURCHASES HAVE NOT GONE OUT OF FASHION DURING THE CAR RIDE HOME.

"Now," continued Piggy, "I believe you two were talking about a certain *him* lurking the hallways?"

I really didn't want the whole world knowing about my problems with Beebus, so I brushed it off. "Oh, it's nothing we can't handle, Miss Piggy."

"Yeah." Pasquale gulped. "But, hypothetically speaking, how would you handle some mean brute who was bullying you?"

Piggy chuckled and walked over to Swedish Chef, who happened to be setting up for his cooking show. "How would *moi* handle a bully, you ask?" She chuckled. "Chef, may I trouble you to borrow this ripe watermelon?"

"Wøøstkermøelen, yøøbetcha!" said Chef.

45

"Piggy!" cried Kermit. "I'm not sure that karate chops are the best way to deal with a bully."

"Yeah." I nodded. "Besides, I'd probably end up being the watermelon in that scenario, anyway."

"Look, guys," Kermit said to us. "Here's what I think you should do. You just need to—"

"Mail call!" came a voice from the hallway. It was Beauregard making his rounds.

Piggy ran up to him like an excited puppy. "Where's mine?! *Moi* has been waiting for her daily satchel of fan correspondence. Gimme! Gimme! Gimme!"

Beauregard dug deep in his mail bag. "Uh, Miss Piggy, let's seeeee…Oh, yeah, here's one!" He handed her one tiny piece of mail.

"PLEASE ENJOY HALF OFF ANY TACO PLATTER AT CHIMICHANGA'S TACO EMPORIUM"? ARE YOU KIDDING ME?

"Did we get any mail for Mon Swoon?" I asked. Usually, we get some sort of fan letter, even if it's only addressed to "Occupant."

Beauregard checked his bag. "No, I don't see anything. But, we do have some mail for something called M.E.S.S."

I perked up as Gonzo, Animal, Fozzie, and Scooter ran up to my side. "M.E.S.S.? Cool! That's us! Well, except for Kip and the Emo Shun guys—they aren't here today."

"Well," Beauregard said, pondering. "I guess I can let you have it."

GIMME!!! GIMME!!!

Beauregard reached out and pulled a rope and a huge mail chute lowered from the ceiling, unleashing a half ton of fan letters on us. We were buried in seconds!

Kermit walked up and opened one of the letters. "Guys! This is all fan mail praising your song 'Girl, Don't Be Rash'!"

"Hmmmmph!" Miss Piggy grumbled and marched off to her dressing room.

SOMETHING TELLS ME THIS POISON IVY SONG MIGHT BE TAKING OFF.

It was pretty obvious that we needed to discuss our newfound success with M.E.S.S., so all the band members gathered in Kermit's office. We even had Kip participate through SKRYPE on Pasquale's laptop.

WE MAY HAVE TO CUT THIS SHORT.

HEY! DON'T START BARKING ORDERS, MASTER COMPUTER!

NO, I WAS TALKING TO MY HAIRSTYLIST. I'M AT THE SALON AS WE SPEAK, YO.

"Hi-ho, everybody," said Kermit. "Thank you all for joining me, and a special thanks to Kip, who is coming to us live via computer from his barbershop."

"Let's start with the bangs," said Kip.

"Yes, I always like to start my meetings off with a

bang," Kermit continued. "As you may have heard, the M.E.S.S. song was used in the Ivy League Poison Ivy Itch Crème commercial last night, and it has become a huuuge hit. Did everybody see the commercial?"

Gonzo raised his hand. "I saw it, and I felt soothed and salved just hearing that song in the background."

"I heard it's already gone viral," said Pasquale.

THEN THANK THE GOODNESS IT IS A COMMERCIAL FOR MEDICATED CREAM, OKAY.

"I like the part in the middle, yo," said Kip over the computer.

"Yes, Kip," agreed Kermit. "The middle of the commercial was very exciting with the knights brandishing back-scratchers."

"Uh, I was actually talking to my stylist," said Kip. "My bad. Carry on."

"Okay," Kermit said, nodding. "Now, does anyone think the commercial could be better?"

"It could use some comedy," suggested Fozzie.

"Do you know any good poison ivy jokes?" I asked.

HOW DO PIGS TREAT POISON IVY? WITH A SOOTHING OINKMENT! WOCKA! WOCKA!

WATCH IT, BEAR!

Kermit brought out a stack of scripts and plopped them in front of us. "The reason I ask is because M.E.S.S. has been asked to perform 'Girl, Don't Be Rash' live in person in the next commercial. I have copies of the script right here."

"It could use trimming," barked Kip.

"I know, the script looks a little long," said Kermit, "but it'll be under a minute. Don't you worry."

"No, I mean my right sideburn, yo," said Kip. "It needs trimming. Forget I said anything. Carry on."

I jumped in. "This is so cool, Kermit! But I think

since things are moving so quickly, it would be foolish if we didn't address the elephant in the room."

"Now that that's taken care of," I continued, "I think it is apparent that we need to make a whole M.E.S.S. album."

"I agree," Scooter said, nodding, "but we need to be careful that we don't oversaturate the market."

"Or the carpet, okay," added Pepe.

"We've got to strive to make sure every song is as memorable as this one," I said.

"Just watch the length in the back and accentuate the highlights," ordered Kip.

"That's right," said Kermit. "Keep the album short and sweet. Good advice, Kip!"

"Actually, I was…oh, never mind." On the screen, I saw Kip shrug.

Scooter brought out a stack of papers. "We should hire a lawyer to look over these contracts. Doing a whole album could entail a lot of wrangling, what with the two boy bands joining forces and all."

"Yeah, it could be tricky," I said. "But I believe it would be worth it for everyone involved."

"Oh, good." Kermit smiled. "Then it's settled. We'll get everything in order and try to do the commercial during spring break, when you kids are out of school. Now, let's get to another important—"

A calamitous *crash* interrupted Kermit as the door of his office was kicked in. When the dust settled, Beaker—or should I say Robo-Beaker—walked into the room, clanging with every step.

"Beaker, you look terrific!" exclaimed Gonzo. "Who is your stylist?"

"My guess is either Vera Klang or Black and Drecker! Wocka! Wocka!" joked Fozzie.

Dr. Honeydew shook his head and said, "I'm afraid Beaker was fused with a litany of kitchen appliances and, much like young Danvers here, we have yet to reverse his condition."

Suddenly Beaker's head started to vibrate, steam seeped out of his mouth, and a high-pitched, headsplitting whistle assaulted our eardrums.

"What is that awful sound?" Piggy shouted, covering her ears.

"Oh, sorry," said Dr. Honeydew, reaching up and removing Beaker's head. "I put some water on to boil before we arrived."

WOULD ANYONE ELSE CARE FOR A CUP OF CHAMOMILE TEA?

IF ANYONE HAS A GOOD "I'M A LITTLE TEAPOT" JOKE, NOW IS THE TIME.

After Dr. Honeydew replaced Beaker's head, I walked up and patted Beaker on the back, sending a slice of toast shooting from his mouth. "I feel a little sorry for the metal guy," I said. "We're kindred spirits. Both transformed into something we can't control and don't know why."

"Hurbde durn burnit byort de bøørbit!" shouted Swedish Chef as he stepped through the shattered door. He was struggling to open a big can of tomatoes. He took one look at Robo-Beaker and said,

"Wøøt de høøey?!" Then he slapped the can under Beaker's nose and pressed down on his head.

SPIN DER TURMATEE UN DE ELECTRY KAANDEE ØØRPENDUR!

Everyone was impressed. "You guys make a great pair!" said Gonzo.

"Yeah, Chef," joked Fozzie. "Beaker could be your opening act! Wocka! Wocka!"

"That's a great idea!" said Kermit. "Beaker, why don't you help Swedish Chef film his cooking show today?"

I was down with that idea. "That would be awesome! Since Beaker is the coolest culinary gadget since the Georgio Forearm Grill, we could film an episode of *The Swedish Chef* with Beaker as the chef's assistant."

Dr. Honeydew perked up. "What a splendid idea!

Until we can figure out how to reverse Beaker's condition, we can at least make the best of the situation."

> OR AT LEAST WE CAN EXPLOIT HIM FOR A FEW CHEAP GAGS!

Swedish Chef took Robo-Beaker by the arm and shouted, "Øønwurd tur de kitchee!" and off they marched.

I walked up to Pasquale and sighed. "Sometimes I feel the same way, Pasquale. Like I'm just making the best of the situation until my condition is reversed. But I'm starting to wonder if there's ever gonna be a reversal in my future. It's like Beaker and I are one and the same."

"I don't know. I think Beaker's got you beat." Pasquale smiled. "He's got a built-in waffle iron."

"What an incredible new look!" beamed Gonzo after Chef and Beaker had left. "Toaster ovens everywhere are going to be clamoring after him."

Pepe agreed, "He look like de metal muffler guy at Alfonzo's Discount Auto Parts, okay."

"It's like he's been transformed into a superhero or something," added Pasquale.

What Pasquale said hit me like a flaming frying pan to the noggin.

"I don't know," said Kermit. "Aren't superheroes supposed to be able to leap tall buildings?"

"Yeah," said Piggy. "You're a terrific kid, but I certainly haven't noticed any superhero qualities. No offense. Except for *moi*'s work as a supermodel, I'm not sure anyone in this room has any superhuman abilities."

"I beg to differ!" shouted Gonzo. "Would any normal non-superhero be able to do this?"

"I rest my case," said Piggy.

"But what other explanation could there be?" I said. "This felty complexion, flip-top mouth, and these wobbly arms were bestowed on me for a reason—I know it. I just have to uncover my super abilities so I can use them for the powers of good. I will rescue the downtrodden, protect fair maidens, lock up perpetrators, collect delinquent library book late charges, and defend my fellow man!"

Pasquale clutched my shoulder. "Okay, dude, but first you need to go home and relax—you know, think this through."

"Correction. I've gotta get home to work on my costume," I declared. Finally, things were starting to make sense to me.

As I left the theater triumphantly, I barely noticed the mob of screaming girls waiting for M.E.S.S. outside.

put on your virtual reality goggles and metallic pants and prepare yourselves for...
The Swedish Chef and Muppet Labs present
KITCHEN OF THE FUTURE
Greetings science and culinary pioneers! today the worlds of technology and gourmet cooking collide as I introduce The Swedish Chef to the Robo-Beaker 3000.
M.E.E.P.
Verdee! Hürdee yürrdøø?
Actually, I wouldn't shake hands if I were you.
ØØPSIE!
Robo-Beaker has super-heated waffle irons for hands.
ØØCHEE! DE Slåpee-slååp makeée de wåflee bøø bøø!
Robo-Beaker 3000 comes equipped with many useful features, like this egg timer proboscis.
un dees blendeé BLØØNDER!
un dee juicee squishee shpitzer!

That night I was a jittery, nervous mess. I wanted so badly to tell my family that I was actually a superhero with superhuman abilities, but I knew that in every comic book ever made, the hero usually keeps his identity a secret—I think it has something to do with an alternating ego.

"Are you okay, Danvers?" my mom asked. "You look very fidgety over there."

"Of course I'm okay," I answered. "I'm just so anxious to try this delicious meat loaf you cooked up."

"Why thank you," my mom said, blushing. "It's a new recipe. I filled the center with creamed spinach."

When I sliced into the cold, gray block of meat, chunky green goop oozed out.

"Now, Chloe," my dad scolded. "We don't talk about barf at the dinner table, no matter how much our food resembles it."

Mom tried to change the subject. "Did you kids do anything interesting today at school?"

"Oh, you know, the usual," I said. Then I shot Chloe an angry look and continued, "I think Chloe might have done something very interesting, though. Something that might be weighing on her conscience?"

"What's a conshence, big bwudda?" she asked with innocent angel eyes.

I wasn't going to let her off the hook. "Stop it with the baby-talk routine. Admit it! You talked Kip into recording that goo-goo, gaga baby album just to humiliate him."

Chloe just shrugged. "People would pay big money for caweer advice from a pwo like me."

"She has a point, Danvers," said Dad. "Chloe *is* singing the new Fluffleberry theme song, and don't forget her solo performance at the Block City Metropolitan Opera."

I couldn't believe they were buying her malarkey. "Come on. It's obvious she did it just to make Kip and his band look like chumps. How could they ever be cool again if the rest of the school heard them singing 'The Wheels on the Bus Go Right Round, Yo'?"

"I wuv that song," Chloe sighed.

"I don't think there is anything wrong with reinventing yourself," said Mom. "People do it all the time. Just look at Uncle Scrooge."

AND WHAT ABOUT SCUFF SHINBONE, THE FORMER LEAD SINGER OF METAL SKELETON? HE'S A SHOE SALESMAN NOW AND, APPARENTLY, FINDS IT VERY REWARDING.

With all the talk of reinventing yourself, my mind started swirling with thoughts about my true destiny, my reason for being, and my new secret identity. I couldn't resist the temptation to spill the beans anymore.

"All right, enough!" I shouted, standing up. "I have an announcement to make. Everyone gather on the sofa."

Once I had my family in the living room, staring at me in rapt attention, I said, "What I'm about to tell you will make your hair stand on end and your jaws drop, and you'll spit your beverages across the room in stunned amazement."

"Not over my new carpet," Mom said, confiscating everyone's glasses of cranberry juice.

That's when I launched into my presentation, using well-thought-out logic, reason, pie charts, a

Pointy Point presentation, and action figures rigged with firecracker explosives, and then finishing with several lines from the Pledge of Allegiance, all leading up to my big reveal:

My revelation was obviously too much for mere mortals to contemplate.

"Isn't anyone gonna say something?" I said to my stunned family.

"Shouldn't superheroes be able to leap buildings or something?" asked Mom.

"Yes," Dad agreed. "No offense, son, but you had trouble just leaping the hurdles in last year's track meet."

"Don't you guys get it?" I pleaded. "I was transformed for a reason. This felty skin, feathery hair, and flip-top mouth were given to me to serve some purpose, and I believe that purpose was to do good."

I BEWEEVE YOU, BIG BWUDDA. I THINK THE WHOLE WORLD SHOULD SEE YOU IN TIGHTS AND A CAPE AS SOON AS POSSIBLE.

"Ooooh!" I huffed. "This is hopeless!" I grabbed Curtis and stormed upstairs to my room.

For about fifteen minutes I just stewed in my own frustration, lying on my bed, staring up at my Gonzo posters. (It should be noted that I hold the world record for the number of Gonzo posters in one kid's room. And those are just the ones on the wall—I've got an extra storage locker filled with 'em.)

"Oh, Gonzo," I called out to a poster of him wakeboarding on a river of cheese. "Why am I like this? What does life have in store for me?"

WHY DO YOU STILL TALK TO YOUR GONZO POSTERS WHEN YOU COULD JUST CALL HIM ON THE PHONE?

Chloe had a point, but I wasn't in any mood to put up with her. "Can't you just leave me alone?" I grumbled. "Don't you have a Fluffleberry that needs grooming?"

"Not when there's a superhero who needs my help," snapped Chloe, whipping out her scissors and glitter.

"And how could you possibly help me?" I smirked.

"Fashion sense, brother. I've got it. You don't."

"What's wrong with my fashion sense?"

"A different color Gonzo shirt for each day of the week is not fashion sense. It's fashion *nonsense.* Now, get up outta that bed and let's accessorize!"

Against my better judgment, I let Chloe dress me with a whole bunch of sparkly super duds.

We finally settled on the outfit—cape, shirt, tights, and boots—but I still needed a mask to protect my identity (and save me from utter humiliation when I went out in public in those blasted pink tights).

"I have the perfect thing," Chloe said, slapping two fluffy donuts with pink icing on my face.

THEY'RE PERFECT! THE ICING KEEPS THEM GLUED TO YOUR FACE AND BRINGS OUT THE PINK IN YOUR TIGHTS.

WHOA! I THINK MY EYES ARE GLAZED OVER. GET IT? *GLAZED* OVER?

PLEASE DON'T TALK WHILE I'M WORKING.

After the ensemble was complete, it was time for the real fun to begin: building my gadgets. Chloe dug into her arsenal of glue sticks, glitter guns, poster paints, sequins, and Popsicle sticks.

"Let's do this," she said. "First, we'll make this grappling-hook launcher out of a ukulele, a jump rope, and a toilet plunger," said Chloe. "Then we will construct battle armor out of these old egg cartons— bedazzled by me, of course."

I looked over at Curtis, who was gnawing on a Cheezy-Q. "Hmmm. I think we should give this to my partner in crime-fighting."

I strapped the camera to the top of Curtis's head and made him a cool outfit out of a black dress sock.

Then it was time to unveil my new look to my folks.

NEVER FEAR, PARENTAL UNITS! IT IS I, DAREDANVERS! AND THIS IS MY PARTNER, SIDE DISH!

My mom looked up calmly from her magazine. "Please tell me you didn't ruin a perfectly good dress sock."

"Never fear! I lost the other one months ago! Now, forgive me—I have crime to fight."

I decided to take my new identity for a test run.

Journal of a Superhero
by ~~Danvers Blickens~~ DareDanvers

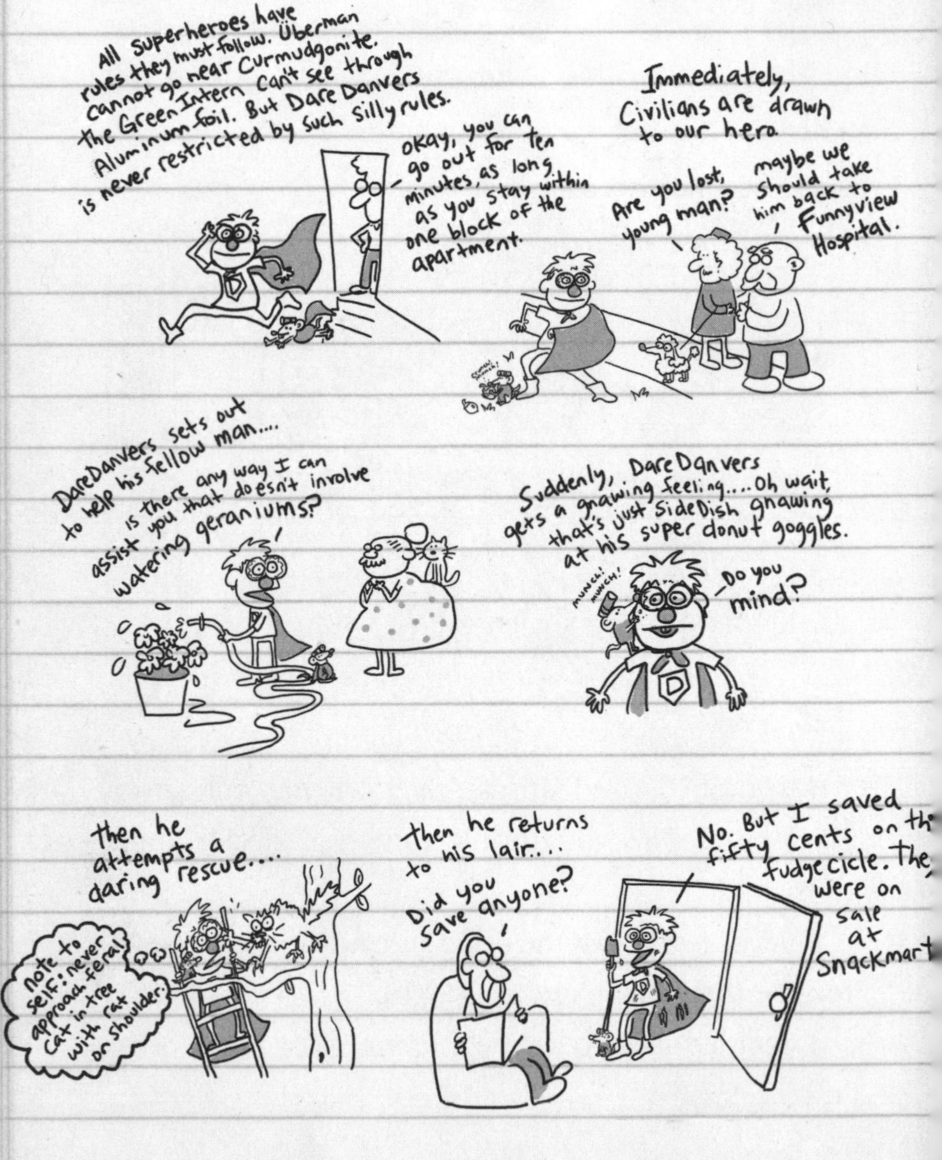

Pasquale was a lot peppier at school

the next morning. I couldn't wait to show him my DareDanvers outfit, which I had stuffed in my backpack. Things seemed just as right as rain.

But I was still a nervous wreck. I just knew that at any moment Beebus would be coming around the corner to make my life miserable.

I made it through Mr. Piffle's class just fine. Well, except for when Mr. Piffle called on me during his Columbus lecture.

DANVERS, WHAT WERE THE THREE SHIPS COLUMBUS SAILED WITH WHEN HE DISCOVERED AMERICA?

UHHHHHHH . . . THE *MARIO*, THE *LUIGI*, AND THE *RATATOUILLE*?

I survived the first half of the day pretty much unscathed. My next class was P.E. and, luckily, it was taught by Coach Kraft—aka Angry Muscle Mountain. Don't worry, he knows about his nickname. He overheard me using it once.

If Beebus tried to give us any grief in Coach Kraft's presence, Coach would eat Beebus for breakfast. Trust me—I've seen Coach eat some pretty weird things for breakfast.

Pasquale and Kip and I changed into our smelly gym clothes and made our way to the basketball court. Beebus was waiting with the rest of the class.

"Niiice legs, Danvers!" He chuckled. "Those things

look like overcooked linguine noodles dipped in orange fuzz!"

He was one to talk, with his legs that looked like blotchy whisker-covered tree trunks. But I kept my mouth shut and looked around. "Where's Coach?" I asked Pasquale.

"I dunno," he said, shrugging.

Kip leaned over and whispered, "Check out behind the bleachers, yo."

I looked over at the bleachers and caught a glimpse of someone's rear sticking out. Kip and I slowly snuck up and crawled under the bleachers to find...

I couldn't believe it. Beebus had Coach Kraft shaking in his way-too-high tube socks.

"Snap out of it, Coach!" I said, shaking him by the shoulders. "How could a little kid like Beebus get you in such a tizzy?"

"Little kid?" cried Coach. "He's no little kid. He's evil in gym shorts! Some say he wasn't even born to human parents but just crawled straight out of a volcanic crater. Others say he was coughed up from the belly of a sea serpent! And many believe he's a curse brought upon us when archaeologists opened a sacred tomb in Egypt!"

"What did he do to you, yo?" asked Kip.

Coach got all quivery and emotional. "It was six years ago. He was in kindergarten. He came into my class with an evil grin on his mug. I was scrawny and weak and he...he...he...he..."

"He what?" I asked.

"He tied my shoelaces together! It was horrible! I fell on my back in front of the whole class, and they laughed at me!"

"That's it?" said Kip. "I was expecting something a little more epic."

"That wasn't it!" Coach blubbered. "Three years went by. I started working out. I went from a scrawny twig of a man to a bulbous slab of pulsating muscle, just in case I ever saw him again.

"Then, in third grade, I had him in my P.E. class again. He still had that evil grin, but was no match for my intimidating brawniness. Then, in the middle of my lecture on stretching your glutes, he… he…he…he…"

"All right, already! He what?" I snapped.

"He tied my shoelaces together again!"

"Again, yo?" said Kip. "That's weak!"

"And this time, it was worse," cried Coach. "I fell on my back, and I was so muscled up and swollen that I couldn't get up. I just flailed around like a june bug that's rolled over! It was horrible!"

Coach's story was pretty disturbing, but I knew all too well the evils that Beebus was capable of. Suddenly, we heard Pasquale call out for help.

Kip and I peeked out through the cracks in the bleachers to see what the commotion was.

I was fuming mad. "Fozzie Bear would have rejected that pun in a heartbeat! This situation calls for DareDanvers!" I said as I unzipped my backpack. It was time to unveil my true self!

"Dare what, yo?" asked Kip. "Dude, why are you taking off your clothes? Are those pink tights, yo?"

I ignored Kip, finished my quick change, and jumped into the basketball court.

STOP YOUR BULLYING NONSENSE THIS INSTANT! AND GET PASQUALE DOWN FROM THAT BASKETBALL HOOP OR ELSE!

Beebus hurled a basketball at Pasquale, knocking him off the basket. "That should count as a three-pointer!" He cackled.

"You'll pay for that!" I shouted. I ran toward Beebus, my cape fluttering in the wind almost in slow motion. Then, I leapt into the air like a mighty condor, my mighty Muppet fist reared back, ready to strike like Thor's hammer. Then...

Luckily, the bell finally rang, or else he really might have embarrassed me.

"You'll pay for this, Beebus!" I warned him. "One of these days you'll get what's coming to ya!"

Beebus just laughed and ripped off one of my doughnut super goggles.

OH, AND BY THE WAY, YOUR COSTUME IS DELICIOUS!

I was crushed, literally and emotionally. My superhero theory was not working out so well.

"What was I thinking, anyway?" I sighed. "How could floppy arms, a removable nose, felty skin, and a flip-top mouth be considered superpowers?"

"Don't let him get to you," Pasquale said. "He's not worth it. I do appreciate your attempt at bravery, although we have to talk about those pink tights."

The other kids in class were kinda confused about my outfit as well.

"Don't worry, dude," added Kip. "In a few days, we leave for spring break. You can relax, refresh, clear your mind, and, hopefully, become a seventh-level black-belt karate champ by the time you get back. Otherwise, this angry ape's gonna turn you into sandwich spread, yo."

"That's *if* I come back from spring break," I said.

Suddenly, Pasquale erupted. "There you go again! Just say it! You wanna go to Eagle Talon Academy! Say it!"

He was really putting me on the spot. Part of me really wanted to go, but the rest of me was scared to commit. I weighed the pluses and minuses in my brain.

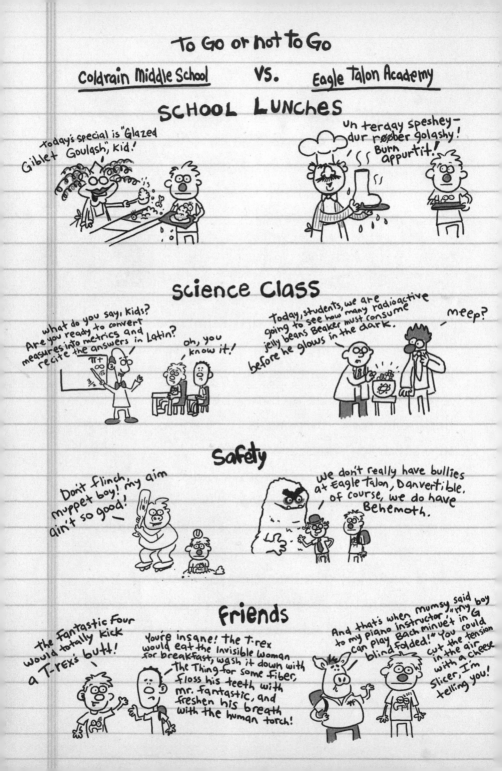

There were good and bad things about both schools—well, maybe it was more like bad and more bad—but I knew in my heart that I wanted to try something new. It pained me to break the news to Pasquale.

So I ended up just blurting it out: "I wanna go to Eagle Talon Academy. And not just because of Beebus, although he helped me make my decision when he filled my ears with baked beans at lunch yesterday. I wanna go there so I can be all the Muppet I can be."

Pasquale didn't believe me. "You're just doing it to run away from your problems!"

"Just settle down, Pasquale," I said, trying to comfort him. "We'll still have our Muppet internship and you'll still be my safety officer."

He stormed off and I suddenly felt horrible—and not just because I had been recently tied into a knot.

"He just needs some time, yo," said Kip.

That's when I noticed something scurrying up to us. It looked kinda like a book, but with skinny legs and antennae.

"What are you doing here, yo?" asked Kip.

"I come to give some exciting news, okay!" Pepe beamed. "But much like the recipe for buttered toast, it is top secret, okay!"

"Uh, everyone knows the recipe for buttered toast," I said.

"Don't bore me with the minor details, okay. Just make sure you are at the internship today, okay. I have made an incredible deal that will rocket you to the stardom, okay! *Ciao!*"

When we all gathered at the Muppet

Theater, I looked around, hoping to spot Pasquale. But he was nowhere to be seen.

"Don't worry, dude," said Kip. "He'll come to his senses, yo."

"It's just a bummer," I said, sighing. "I mean, just look at what Pasquale is missing."

GONZO! WHY IS THE LOBBY CRAWLING WITH ACCORDION-PLAYING STINKBUGS?

THOSE ARE FOR MY BIG NUMBER, "SMELL AND THE WHOLE WORLD SMELLS WITH YOU"! I'M PERFORMING IT IN STINK-O-RAMA.

"Yep," said Kip. "He's missing out on some true genius in action."

That was when Kermit gathered everyone around

and said, "Okay, folks! Quiet down. As you may have heard, we have a big announcement regarding our own huge M.E.S.S., so take it away, Pepe and Rizzo!"

"Take what away?" asked Pepe.

"Make your announcement!" whispered Kermit.

"Ohhhh, okay, okay!" Pepe continued. "*Holaaaa*, my friends! As you may not know, I am the publicizer for our new super boy band. Because it is so popular, okay, I have asked Rizzo to help me out with this M.E.S.S."

FIRST WE WANNA ANNOUNCE THESE NEW KILLER IRON-ONS. NOW, IN JUST MINUTES, YOU CAN HAVE A M.E.S.S. ON YOUR T-SHIRT!

OR, YOU MAY PREFER TO M.E.S.S. YOUR PANTS, OKAY.

"That's it?" Miss Piggy huffed, arms folded. "Surely you interrupted *moi*'s Tunisian pedicure for something more exciting than decals."

"Yes, guys," prodded Kermit. "Tell everyone about the next commercial."

"Commercial, ha!" scoffed Rizzo. "We've got

an announcement that will make the medicated-ointment commercial look like a, uh...like a...I dunno—what's lower than a medicated-ointment commercial?"

"Maybe a commercial for the Snug-It blanket for poodles, okay," whispered Pepe.

"Will you guys please just get to the point?!" Kermit flailed.

"Okay," Rizzo continued. "You know that reality show on the Aw Naturale Network *My Life with a Polar Bear*? Well, we just got wind that the show has been suddenly canceled."

"What happened?" I asked.

LET'S JUST SAY THE POLAR BEAR GOT HUNGRY, OKAY.

THEY SHOULD HAVE FILMED THAT SHOW WITH ME. WHEN I GET HUNGRY, I USUALLY JUST GO FOR SOME GRAHAM CRACKERS.

SNIFF SNIFF

MY LIFE WITH A POLAR BEAR

"What this means," added Rizzo, "is that there is an open slot in the TV schedule that needs to be filled, and we just agreed to shoot a Muppet special TV movie to air in its place!"

Kermit looked stunned. "You probably shouldn't have done that, guys."

"We know. We know, okay," Pepe said. "We shouldn't have. But we wanted to, okay. It is the least we could do to repay the froggy green guidance you have given us, okay."

"We also promised them we would be done with it in time for the next episode," said Rizzo.

Kermit looked like he was going to have a heart attack. "Guys! Casting, planning, shooting, and editing take a lot of time!"

Rizzo patted Kermit on the arm. "We know that! That's why we told them we couldn't possibly be done until the end of next week."

"NEXT WEEK?!" Kermit cried. "We can't finish it in one week!"

"I think we kinda have to." Rizzo gulped. "We already signed the contract. We couldn't help it. They treated us to all-you-can-eat banana splits at Ice Cream Meltdown. You know that place makes us weak."

Kermit started swaying like he was going to faint. Kip and I propped him up.

"I know this all sounds too good to be true," Pepe said. "But there is a catch."

"A catch?" blared Piggy. "You mean it gets worse?"

"The producers want it to be a summer band-camp musical set in the great outdoors," said Rizzo. "You know, since it's on the Aw Naturale Network, and also to go along with the poison ivy song. And, they want Kip and Danvers to be the stars and sing 'Girl, Don't Be Rash' in the big finale."

"Who's gonna provide funding?" Scooter asked.

"No sweat!" Rizzo said, presenting Scooter with a signed check. "Our new buds at Ivy League Itch Crème have provided a budget that you will find shocking, I guarantee."

Scooter took one look at the check and cried, "Yikes! This budget couldn't even cover lunch."

"See," said Rizzo. "I knew it would shock you."

Fozzie walked up to me. "What do you think, Danvers? No more reality shows. This is a real TV movie! You're gonna be an even bigger celebrity!"

But I was incapable of speaking. Little gold stars were swirling around me, my eyes were filled with dollar signs, and Hollywood spotlights were shining all over the room—just like in some cheesy illustration in a middle-grade book.

At dinner that night, I was so excited

I could barely eat—which probably saved my life, since my mom was trying out her latest meat-loaf recipe.

SINCE YOU GUYS WEREN'T TOO KEEN ON THE LAST MEAT LOAF, I REPLACED THE CREAMED-SPINACH CENTER WITH CANNED PEAS.

AW, YOU SHOULDN'T HAVE, MOMMY. WEALLY, I MEAN IT. I MAY HAVE TO WEPORT YOU TO THE AUTHORITIES.

I let everyone settle into their seats and get started on their slop—er, uh, dinner. My plan was to break the big news that I was going to star in my own TV special. I was just about to open my mouth when...

"Kids, your father has a little announcement he'd like to make," my mom said. She had beaten me to the punch.

"That's right," my dad coughed. "As you know, times have been tough. We've had to cut back. You kids have had to share bunk beds."

"Don't remind me," I moaned.

"We must all make sacwifices," Chloe replied. "And I am honored to help sacwifice Danvers's privacy for the good of the family."

My dad continued, "Well, my new job has been a big load off, but now with Danvers about to start private school, we will have to pay through the nose."

"Ick," I said, grimacing. "I hope they wipe off the money afterward."

My folks gave me a stern, silent glare. "Sorry," I said. "It was the Muppet in me talking." It's true. Sometimes I think I need to go to Snappy One-Liners Anonymous.

"I guess what I'm trying to say is," my dad concluded, "I have decided to take a second job at Fryd's Computers and Circuit Boards."

"But that's ridiculous!" I said.

"I know, I know," my dad agreed. "I'll barely have time to see you guys."

"No! I mean the only computer you've ever used was built in the Paleolithic Era!"

"It'll be worth it," my dad said. "I'm willing to learn about all these newfangled floppy-disc drives and intranet telephone cables and virtual realities if it means making my kids happy."

My dad's speech was so heartfelt and honorable that my eyes teared up. Or maybe it was the fumes from my mom's onion, garlic, and raisin gravy.

"Thanks, Dad," I said. I waited a few minutes before launching into my exciting announcement. I stood up and declared, "I also have an announc—"

Ding! Ding! Ding! Ding!

I looked over to see Chloe standing in her chair and dinging her juice cup with a fork.

I AM PWOUD TO ANNOUNCE THAT BECAUSE I COLLECTED THE MOST FLUFFLEBERRY ACTION FIGURE PWOOF OF PURCHASES, I WILL NOT ONLY BE SINGING THE THEME SONG OF *FLUFFLEBERRIES ARE FWEE*, BUT I HAVE BEEN CAST AS THE LEAD IN THE MOVIE AS WELL.

I couldn't believe my ears. My own sister, the lead in a big Hollywood movie! How revolting!

"I will play young Penny Pwimwose, a human space traveler stranded on the world of Plethora. I lead the Fluffleberry webellion against the Insecta-dwoids, venomous slave dwivers from the planet Oozopolis," Chloe continued. "We'll be shooting next week with a budget of infinity, give or take a hundred dollars."

"That's impressive," said my mom. "Maybe your dad won't have to sell computers after all, with this extra income coming in."

"I'll haf to check with Rocko, my money guy, about that," Chloe said. "But I'm sure we can work something out."

"What a shock!" my dad said, laughing. "My own daughter, a movie star. Could this dinner be full of any more surprises?"

It was my turn. There was no way my news was going to sound all that amazing now that Chloe had stolen my thunder, but I tried to make it exciting anyway. "Funny you should ask! It turns out that I, too, will starring in my own production next week during spring break."

I gave them all the nitty-gritty details: the canceled reality show, the summer-camp musical theme, the M.E.S.S. theme song.

"Well," my mom said, taking a deep breath. "This is even more exciting than your superhero announcement. I guess I need to congratulate you, too, Danvers."

"Yes," said Chloe. "I'm sure your itchy ointment pwoject will be charming. I always say it's good to keep busy."

"Wait a minute," Mom interrupted. "You two will have adult chaperones, right?"

"Of course!" bragged Chloe. "I will be sleeping in my own luxury trailer on the set. Plus, I'll have two on-set nannies, a pwivate chef, thwee bodyguards, and a foot masseuse."

"I'll be sleeping in a…uh, run-down cabin in the wilderness," I said.

I ALSO PUT IN A REQUEST FOR FOUR ARMED BODYGUARDS AND, WELL, THEY GAVE ME PEPE.

ONE FOUR-ARMED BODYGUARD AT YOUR SERVICE, OKAY!

It took some convincing, but my folks finally agreed. They wouldn't let me go see PG-13 movies, but sending me off to some campground to shoot a movie for a whole week with Pepe as my protector was just fine. Go figure!

Whether we were ready or not, our TV movie was a go! The budget was so tight that, well, let's just say my mom and dad pay me the same amount to take out the trash every week. Kermit wasn't going to be able to hire some fancy screenwriter to whip out a script, so he gave the job to Fozzie and Rizzo. Scooter would be his right-hand man, Rowlf would compose the score, Gonzo would work as stunt coordinator, and everything else would be handled by...

SHEESH. THERE IS NO ONE ELSE. GUESS I'LL HAVE TO DO IT.

First up was casting. Kermit convinced Sam Eagle, principal of Eagle Talon Academy and proud patriot, to hold the auditions for the summer-camp musical in his school auditorium. Eagle Talon is crawling with kid talent, and I'm sure Kermit wanted to take advantage of that, but Sam was reluctant. For some reason, he had it in his head that summer-camp movies are all gross and juvenile—probably because of the hugely popular Camp Stinkhorn series.

Man, I love those movies.

"Sorry, Kermit. I couldn't possibly allow this fine institutions to be involved in such a disreputable genre," huffed Sam. "Think of the children."

"But, Sam," said Kermit. "The children are exactly why we need you. I want you to play the fearless camp leader, Stern Hozen. Your wise and seasoned expertise will keep this project from resorting to tasteless jokes and sinking into the sewer."

PERHAPS YOU'RE RIGHT. MOST SUMMER-CAMP MOVIES ARE FILLED WITH VULGARITY AND BASE HUMOR. WITH MY GUIDANCE, THIS FILM WILL BECOME A CAMP CLASSIC.

OH, GOOD! I'M GLAD TO HAVE YOU ON BOARD.

"Hey, Kermit!" Rizzo yelled, running in with Fozzie. "We just wrote a hilarious scene in the script where Camp Leader Hozen sinks into the sewer!"

"I beg your pardon," gasped Sam.

"Never mind about that. We're still fine-tuning the script," said Kermit. He whipped out a bullhorn and announced, "Attention, everyone! Auditions start in ten minutes!"

"Ten minutes?" Sam protested. "Now, wait just a sec—"

The auditorium doors swung open and kids started flooding in.

"What have I gotten myself into?" Sam sighed.

Over in the corner, Rizzo and Fozzie were busy typing the script. "How's the screenwriting coming?" I asked.

"It's great!" said Rizzo. "Fozzie and I make a great team. He writes the gags and I erase them and add my own."

The joint quickly filled up with applicants and Kermit ran out onstage to get the ball rolling. "Hi-ho, everybody! Welcome to the tryouts for our

latest, greatest, we're-only-making-this-because-we-
are-legally-obligated-to production of *Camp Muppet*.
Yaaaaaaaaaay!!! I'll be judging the auditions along
with Miss Piggy and Rowlf!"

AND WE'LL BE PROVIDING DESTRUCTIVE CRITICISM!

DARN! I KNEW THIS JOB DESCRIPTION SOUNDED TOO GOOD TO BE TRUE!

I THINK IT'S SUPPOSED TO BE *CONSTRUCTIVE* CRITICISM!

Kip and I watched from backstage with Gonzo
and the rest of the gang. "Man, I wish Pasquale
could be part of this," I said, sighing.

"So do I!" said Gonzo. "Who's gonna make sure I
don't get pulverized into blue mulch during my big
stunt?"

LET ME JUST BEGIN WITH A BRIEF SYNOPSIS OF THE SCRIPT. IT BEGINS ON A BEAUTIFUL DAY AT . . . ACTUALLY, I DON'T HAVE A SCRIPT YET. GUYS, WHERE'S THE SCRIPT?

"Sorry, Kermit," said Fozzie from the side of the stage. "Here, catch!" He hurled the script to Kermit.

"Sheesh!" Kermit frowned. "Starting a shoot without a complete script. This would never happen on a big Hollywood production." He shook his head and started reading a synopsis of the script.

"*Camp Muppet* is the story of two kids at summer band camp vying for the affection of the girl of their dreams while competing in the camp talent show, dealing with a big bully, and commanding a force of ten thousand warriors in an epic coconut-cream-pie fight with a battalion of orcs in clown makeup? Uh, guys? We don't have the budget for an army of orcs."

"Sorry," said Fozzie. "I got a little carried away with that last part."

"The first role we will audition is the part of Dragun Uckles, the big bully galoot who makes everyone's life miserable. Let the audition begin!"

I went out onstage to help the applicants act out their scenes.

All of your friends are at the soda shop, drinking sarsaparilla. No one can save you now, my fair maiden! Heh! Heh! Heh!
Curses! Foiled again!
I don't know. This seems a little old-fashioned.
Director, what's my motivation for this scene? My instructor at Carlsbad Acting Academy said a performer must know his motivation before perform...
Neeext.

All right, buster! I'm gonna beat you up and... Awwww, Kermit, I'm sorry! I can't do it! I'm just a big softy. Don't you have any nice parts I can play?
Well, he sure looked the part. Just goes to show, you can't judge a book by its cover.
Tell me about it! The cover of this book promised it was going to be funny! Ha Ha!

Are you looking at me, okay? Why are you looking at me? I coulda been a contender! All I ever wanted to do all my life was dance, okay! But you can't handle the truth! No one ever puts de baby in the corner, okay! And may the force be with—
Okay, thanks, Pepe. That was very.... uh, thorough.
I never knew they could pack that much ham in such a small package!
I'll give you five seconds - rephrase tha

It was exhausting but kinda fun to help out with the auditions. I have to admit I was getting a little sore from all these wannabe bullies shaking me around. But they were all a walk in the park compared to the next contestant.

"The next person trying out is from Coldrain Middle School," said Kermit, reading from his call sheet. "He enjoys moonlit walks on warm summer nights, Shakespeare in the Park, and helping less fortunate kids manage their lunch money. Ladies and gentlemen, I give you Beebus Spracklin!"

I couldn't believe my eyes. My worst nightmare was snorting his stinky, hot breath down on me.

"Uhhhh…" I turned to Kermit. "I thought we were just auditioning kids from Eagle Talon Academy?"

"Oh, no." Kermit smiled. "I want everyone to have a chance to participate. Folks from schools all over the city, actors, non-actors, even Crazy Mo from Crazy Mo's Beard-Trimmer Emporium is going to try out."

I WANNA PLAY A BALLERINA, DAB NABBIT!

"All right, Beebus," Kermit directed. "Let's see what you've got."

"Don't worry. I'll be as gentle as a lamb," Beebus said, grabbing me. Then he twirled me in the air like a lasso, shook me like a pillowcase full of corn-flakes, slammed me back and forth on the stage like a wet towel, and, finally, tied me into his signature pretzel knot.

Kermit stood up. "Is everything okay up there?"

Beebus leaned close and whispered, "I want this part, so keep your flip-top mouth shut or you know those regularly scheduled wedgies you get on Tuesdays and Thursdays?"

"Yeah." I gulped.

"I might just have to make those an everyday occurrence. And I'll include your friend Pasquale in the deal, too."

I turned to Kermit and said, "Everything's great, Kermit! It didn't hurt a bit! I think we've found our Dragun Uckles!"

Kermit relaxed. "Whew! That looked so convincing. What a performance! Well, that's settled. Beebus is our bad guy."

"This is an outrage, okay!" shouted Pepe. "Everyone knows that I am much more intimidating and brawny, okay!"

"More like *prawny!*" shouted Statler.

Backstage, Kip helped me untangle my arms. "Dude, yo," he said. "You gotta tell Kermit that Beebus is a real bully. He can't put him in our TV show. It just ain't right."

"Don't worry about it," I said, brushing him off. "I can handle that big oaf. Besides, he earned that role. Have you ever seen a more convincing orangutan?"

Kip wasn't satisfied. "If you don't tell Kermit, then I w—"

Suddenly, Kip stopped gabbing. He froze in place, and his mouth fell open like a bear trap. I turned to look at what had caught his attention, and pretty soon my jaw joined Kip's on the floor. Any thoughts of big Beebus quickly left my brain as the most glorious vision I've ever, uh, envisioned rolled in from stage right on a bright pink skateboard, did a kick flip, and stopped next to Kermit.

SORRY I'M LATE. I WAS AT ELECTRIC-GUITAR PRACTICE, THEN I HAD TO SKATE ALL THE WAY UP HANGMAN'S HILL TO GET HERE.

"Oh, no problem!" said Kermit, checking his list of names. "You must be Sofi."

"Totes!" Sofi giggled.

Kermit flipped through his script. "And I bet you're trying out for the part of Lana, the fiery, tough songwriter with a taste for grape licorice and...illegal wombat racing? Who comes up with this stuff?"

NEVER QUESTION THE THOUGHT PROCESS OF A SCREENWRITER.

Kermit asked me to come out onstage to do a scene with Sofi. "Now remember, the audience has to believe that Lana is someone Danvers and Kip would fall so madly head over heels for, they would orchestrate huge musical numbers for her and go head-to-head in the big showdown over her, ultimately threatening their friendship. Now, let's do the scene where Lana shows Danvers the new song she's written."

Kip snapped out of his stupor and rushed out onstage, saying, "Wait a minute, dudes! Shouldn't we do the scene where I sing Lana a romantic ballad by the light of the campfire? It's much more dramatic. I've got my guitar and some extra hair product in my backpack, ready to go, yo."

"No way, *yo!*" I snapped back. "We should do the scene where Lana and I are lost in the woods, with only s'mores and rainwater to keep us alive!"

"Oh, *contraire*, dude! We obviously need to perform the scene where Lana nurses me back to health with Poison Ivy lotion and rattlesnake antivenom!"

I **was buzzing with excitement on** the last day of school before spring break, but I was also nervously trying to avoid running into Beebus—running into him hurts, trust me!

Pasquale was still giving me the cold shoulder, like twenty-five-degrees-below-zero cold, but I wanted to try to make peace with him. Surely he'd come to his senses and want to be part of our movie. But I couldn't find him anywhere.

I spotted Button Hauser near the school trophy cabinet and asked her if she had seen him.

PASQUALE CALLED IN SICK TODAY. HE SAID HE WAS FEELING DISCOMBOBULATED, BUT I SENSE THAT HE WAS HIDING A DEEPER PAIN. THE PAIN OF BEING DESERTED BY SOMEONE HE THOUGHT WAS HIS BEST FRIEND AND LEFT TO FEND FOR HIMSELF IN THE COLD, CRUEL WORLD. OH, I ALMOST FORGOT—WOULD YOU LIKE TO BUY SOME COOKIES?

I bought three boxes of Peanut Butter Kiddie Klumps just because I felt so guilty. And what's worse, I ate half of them on the bus ride home.

It's actually kind of hard to eat cookies when you're a Muppet. Crumbs get everywhere.

That night I was super gloomy as I packed for my film shoot.

"Oh, Curtis," I sighed, stuffing my duffel bag with socks and Gonzo shirts, and stuffing my mouth with Kiddie Klumps. "I should be so jazzed. I've got a hit song, I'm about to enroll in a prestigious academy, and I'm starring in a TV production with the girl of my dreams, but I can't quit thinking about Pasquale."

Curtis gave me a little nibble and curled up in my crazy yellow hair for some shut-eye.

The next morning, my folks joined Chloe and me at the curb outside our apartment, where we were waiting for our rides. They seemed anxious to see us off.

"Are you guys all packed?" said my mom. "You didn't forget anything, did you?"

"Oh, I'm just bringing the basics," I said, pointing to my sad duffel bag on the sidewalk.

I felt a little tug at my shoelace and looked down to see Curtis sitting next to my DareDanvers superhero secret-gadget case.

"I think my superhero days are over, Curtis," I said with a sigh. "It was a noble experiment, but a failed one nonetheless." But Curtis kept tugging at my shoelace and squeaking forcefully.

I finally grabbed the case. "All right! All right! I

guess we might be able to use this in the movie, just to liven the wardrobe up. Man, you are one pushy rat sometimes."

Speaking of pushy rats...my sister was getting ready for her shoot in her own special way. And by "special," I mean "annoying."

WARDROBE, CHECK. MAKEUP MIRROR, CHECK! HYPOALLERGENIC DOWN PILLOW AND COMFORTER, CHECK! PERSONAL INFLATABLE BOUNCE HOUSE, CHECK!

"You packed a little heavy, princess," my dad pointed out. "How do you plan on getting all that to the set?"

Suddenly, we heard the sound of a helicopter overhead, and a hook lowered down.

Chloe latched the hook to her luggage and said, "No pwoblem! The studio hired a chopper to airlift it to the location!"

Then a fancy limousine the length of a party boat pulled up. A chauffeur got out and opened the door for my little sister.

"Gotta be going!" Chloe waved. "They serve bweakfast in the limo pwomptly at eight. Oh, look!" She pointed across the street. "Danvas, your wide is here, too!"

I hugged my parents, grabbed Curtis, and jumped onto the moving bus—with a little help from Animal.

"Cool!" I said to Dr. Teeth once I was safely on board. "I've always wanted to hop onto a moving vehicle, just like in an action flick! That was exciting!"

"If you thought it was fun getting on a bus with no brakes, wait till we drop you off!" Dr. Teeth said, laughing.

I went to the back of the bus and waved to my parents. They looked kind of pitiful on the sidewalk. Like they didn't know what to do with themselves.

"Poor guys," I said to Curtis. "I hope they aren't too bored and lonely without us kids to give their lives purpose."

We drove to the outskirts of town, near some pretty thick, spooky looking woods. As we approached a run-down summer camp, I flung myself from the bus and rolled up to the film crew.

WHAT AN ENTRANCE!

SHEESH! YOU COULD'VE BROKEN YOUR NECKS, JUMPING OUT OF A BUS LIKE THAT!

WELL, AT LEAST IT WAS A NONSTOP FLIGHT WITH ONLY ONE ROLLOVER.

Gonzo and Kermit helped me and Curtis dust ourselves off, and then we joined Kip and the rest of the gang at the entrance to the creepiest, shoddiest, most run-down camp you've ever seen. The place was packed with kids from all over. A lot of our Coldrain classmates had agreed to play extras.

The entrance to the camp was overrun with poison ivy vines, and a dilapidated sign was posted over it, barely hanging on by a couple of rusty nails.

"Dude. This place is gnarly, yo," griped Kip.

"Camp Pain?" I said. "How did you guys find this place?"

"Oh, a lot of us used to come here during the summers when we were younger," said Kermit. "But now it's a little run-down."

"A little?" Kip whispered to me. "If it were any more run-down, it'd be roadkill, yo."

AH, YES. I REMEMBER SPENDING HOURS ON THE CAMP PAIN TRAIL WITH THE YOUNG, IDEALISTIC CAMP PAIN VOLUNTEERS. BUT THEN, AFTER A REGRETTABLE OUTBREAK OF MUDSLINGING, THE CAMP PAIN CONTRIBUTIONS DRIED UP.

WE *ARE* STILL TALKING ABOUT SUMMER CAMP, RIGHT?

I had to be honest with Kermit. "I don't know about the name. Camp Pain just has such negative connotations."

"Hmm…" said Kermit. "You might be right, Danvers. We want the band camp in our production to be happy and positive, and Camp Pain just sounds so…painful."

"Why was it ever called that to begin with, yo?" asked Kip.

I DON'T KNOW. I ALWAYS HAD A GREAT TIME AT CAMP PAIN. JUST LOOK HOW HAPPY I AM IN THIS OLD PHOTO.

"Who are we kidding?" snapped Piggy. "This place was a nightmare! Poison ivy, ticks, thorny vines, polyester camp T-shirts, no cable TV—even the rattlesnakes complained about the brutal conditions!"

Sam looked a little misty-eyed. "Aw, those were the good ol' days. I can still remember the old Camp Pain slogan, 'Survive at all costs. Even if you have to eat your own foot.'"

"You mean, like Bigfoot?" I asked.

"Even worse," said Gonzo. "Big Chicken!"

"Big Chicken?" Kip laughed. "Seriously, yo?"

"Yes!" cried Gonzo. "Big Chicken, the giant poultry that haunts these parts. Some say she's over nine feet tall, with a waddle the size of a recyclable shopping bag and an insatiable appetite for hen scratch. At night, you can see her giblet glowing a ghostly green."

Kermit looked a little irritated. "Gonzo! That's just an old wives' tale."

"That's funny—I first heard it from a teenage muskrat," said Gonzo.

"This is all too gloomy and scary for our movie," I told them. "I say we call this place Camp Muppet! Just like the name of our special."

"But I just changed the name of our special to *Kitty Calypso and the Giant Chocolate Molten Lava Cake of Death*," said Rizzo, clacking on his typewriter.

"We can't afford a giant chocolate lava cake of death, Rizzo," Kermit pointed out. "I think Camp Muppet sounds perfect! We'll have to paint over the old sign, of course."

"That's gonna double the budget, but okay." Pepe shrugged.

Fozzie went ahead and started passing out new scripts. "Here are the new screenplays, everybody. Just ignore the chocolate lava cake finale."

"We added all sorts of cool new stuff," said Rizzo. "Now there's canoeing, sack racing, wild-animal wrangling, spooky campfire stories, dangerous waterskiing stunt shows, and lots of contractually obligated mentions of Ivy League Poison Ivy Itch Crème."

SLATHER THAT RASH WITH PANACHE! USE IVY LEAGUE!

"And we have some casting news, too," Fozzie continued. "Dr. Bunsen Honeydew, you will play the camp nature expert."

SWEDISH CHEF, YOU'LL PLAY THE CAMP COOK, AND IN THE ROLE OF THE TOUGH-AS-NAILS, SEASONED, OLDER, VETERAN DEN MOTHER WILL BE NONE OTHER THAN MISS—

MISS SOMEONE-ELSE-WHO-IS-NOT-MISS-PIGGY BECAUSE *MOI* WILL BE PLAYING THE ROLE OF BECKY LORRAINE, FRESH-OUT-OF-COLLEGE CAMP COUNSELOR AND LOVE INTEREST OF ONE GREEN, DREAMY CAMP LEADER!

"But there is no fresh-out-of-college camp counselor in our script," said Fozzie.

"Well, there is now!" Piggy growled, tossing him her own script. "I made a few revisions and printed copies for everyone."

"Okay, then," Kermit said, pulling out his roll-call clipboard. "Let's see…it looks like we're missing Beebus. Has anyone seen Beebus Spracklin?"

I was secretly kinda hoping that big ogre wouldn't show up.

"I suggest you check under a large rock," I said, under my breath.

"Or maybe in the Dumpster out back," Kip added, giggling.

A huge shadow rose up over us. I knew I had put my foot firmly in my big, floppy mouth. I turned to see Beebus grinning at me like the Cheshire Cat.

"You're such a card, Danvers," Beebus said in his phony nice voice, chuckling. "I'm so glad we're working together. I can't wait to do the scene where I dangle you over a den of water moccasins."

I was doomed. Before this shoot was through, Bee-bus was going to turn me into ground chuck for sure. But even though he was making me incredibly nervous, I was totally preoccupied looking for Sofi. I hadn't seen her yet.

"Dude," said Kip, as desperate to see her as I was. "Where is Sofi? We can't start filming without my love interest, yo."

I laughed. "Ha! Correction—I believe she is *my* love interest."

Suddenly we heard the roar of The Electric Mayhem bus again as it came blaring down the road. "Special delivery!" Dr. Teeth yelled out the window. "One leading lady C.O.D.! That's Crash on Demand!"

As the bus zoomed by, Sofi jumped off and twirled through the air. Kip and I threw ourselves into the mud so she could land on us to cushion her fall, but she pulled out her skateboard in midair and did an amazing double-laser heel flip, then landed next to us.

"Oh, no problem." Kermit said, smiling.

> THAT BUS IS LIKE A BATHTUB THAT WON'T FILL UP...NO *STOPP*ER!

Sofi's beautiful hair was a little mussed from her airborne arrival. "Man. I got some epic bedhead," she said, and giggled.

Kip jumped up and whipped out his secret stash of hair gel.

> WHATEVER YOU NEED, GIRL, I GOT YOUR BACK. THE WHOLE SPECTRUM OF HAIR PRODUCTS, FROM INTENSE HOLD ALL THE WAY UP TO CEMENT-MIX SUPER GRIP, YO.

> AWWW, THANKS! I'LL TRY BRICK MORTAR BOND.

Kip's flirty behavior was already starting to make my felt crawl. How dare he move in on my leading lady!

"I must caution you, folks," Kermit announced. "This will not be an easy shoot. We'll be sleeping in actual camp quarters, eating by the light of the campfire, subsisting on s'mores and freshly captured dragonflies. This is no-frills guerilla filmmaking."

GORILLA? I THOUGHT THE FROG WAS MAKING IT?

NEVER FEAR, KERMIE. *MOI* CAN ADAPT TO ANY SORT OF UNFORGIVING, BRUTAL CONDITIONS FOR HER ART. BEAKER! CAPPUCCINO! PRONTO!

"All right, folks!" said Kermit. "Now that everyone has, uh, dropped in, we can get started. I'll be handling directing, editing, gaffing, and any mountain-goat wrangling. This is all due to a certain prawn and rat, who shall remain nameless."

IT WAS NOTHING. YOU CAN THANK US LATER, OKAY.

CHAPTER 12

CAMP PAIN REGULATIONS

1. No matter how soft and friendly the name Cottonmouth sounds, do not pet them!

2. Check your shoes for spiders. It is where they most like to hang out and set up their entertainment centers.

3. That piercing screech and scraping sound you hear in the middle of the night is merely the skeleton-like branches of the Deadwood Tree, which some say is cursed by the spirits of angry forest gnomes, so there is absolutely nothing to be afraid of.

4. If you step on a rusty nail, poisonous branch, or a flesh-eating-germ-covered pointy thing—never fear, Nurse Big Mean Carl will be there to administer your tetanus shot.

5. Remember—the slightly shiny red berries with the light green polka dots are toxic enough to take down ten water buffalo. The shinier red berries with the dark green polka dots are absolutely delicious and should be eaten like jelly beans. Bon appetit!

With your help, we can make your visit to Camp Pain a survivable one!

(paid for by the Camp Pain finance committee)

"**A**ttention, everybody!" called Kermit. "Before we begin filming, I just want to stress how important safety is during your stay at Camp Pain…er, I mean Camp Muppet. All of your parents want you kids returned to them in one piece, two at the most. Just kidding."

"Ahem!" coughed Sam Eagle. "Safety is no joking matter. As the old camp counselors used to tell us before checking our cabins for rattlesnakes, 'Camp Pain offers a multitude of pleasures and learning opportunities, but it can also be an unending nightmare of danger and agony.'"

"With a sales pitch like that, no wonder the camp went out of business," mumbled Miss Piggy.

Sam pulled out a poster and unrolled it. "I made this helpful safety guide, which I will post next to the pit of broken glass behind the cactus patch. Please heed its advice."

"Man, this place isn't exactly a vacation destination, yo," said Kip.

"More like a final destination." I nodded.

"*Sacre bleu!*" cried Danny.

Seriously, I was starting to think Fozzie and Rizzo should rewrite this production as a horror movie! Dr. Honeydew stepped up to speak next.

With all these safety lessons and dire warnings, I was really starting to get the willies about Camp Muppet. But then I just thought about *her* again. Sofi—that guitar-playing, skateboarding goddess of beauty. Little, cartoon, chubby cherubs swirled around my head, and my heart almost pounded its way out of my Gonzo shirt.

"Okay, folks!" Kermit shouted into his director's bullhorn. "Our very first scene of the day is the one where the two boy bands, Emo Shun and Mon Swoon, watch Lana perform a pop song while skateboarding through a hollowed-out log!"

Fozzie took off his hat and confessed, "Kermit, we didn't have the money for a log. Would you settle for a hollow twig or a paper-towel tube?"

HOW IS SHE SUPPOSED TO SING A POP SONG WHILE SKATING IN A HOLLOW LOG IF WE DON'T HAVE A HOLLOW LOG?

MAYBE SHE COULD TRY SKATING ON A *HARD ROCK*! GET IT? HARD ROCK? WOCKA! WOCKA!

Kermit turned to Scooter. "Scooter, send Beauregard out into the woods. There has to be a hollow log out there somewhere."

"Yes, but they are usually full of vipers," warned Sam.

Miss Piggy walked up, pulled Kermit aside, and said, "Kermie, perhaps this is a sign from the entertainment gods."

"I don't read you, Piggy," Kermit said, shaking his head.

She fluffed her hair like a glamour model. "Maybe we don't need two female leads in such a tiny little teensy-weensy TV special. Isn't one ravishing acting and musical sensation enough?"

BUT, PIGGY, SOFI BRINGS IN THE TWELVE- TO SIXTEEN-YEAR-OLD AUDIENCE. YOU JUST DON'T APPEAL TO THE SAME DEMOGRAPHIC.

THERE IS NO REASON TO BRING POLITICS INTO THIS, OKAY. LET'S KEEP IT CIVIL.

I stepped in to speak up for Sofi. "Yeah, Miss Piggy. And Sofi's, like, the only girl out there that sings and does stunt work at the same time."

Piggy gave me the look an angry bull probably gives a matador just before skewering him. "Ahem! Are you implying that *moi* cannot sing and perform a silly stunt at the same time?"

"Uh...I d-didn't mean anything by that..." I stuttered. I really didn't want to be on the business end of a Piggy karate chop. Not in front of Sofi.

"Gonzo!" Piggy bellowed. "What are you doing right now?"

Gonzo ran up, holding Camilla, his chicken girlfriend. "I'm just preparing the top secret megastunt for the big riverboat finale!"

Kermit called out after her, "You don't have to do a dangerous stunt, Piggy! We love you just the way you are!"

"'Love' is a very strong word, okay," said Pepe.

So, while Beauregard went hollow-log hunting, Kermit came up with a bunch of other stuff we could shoot. It was showtime!

ALL RIGHT! PLACES, EVERYBODY! AS THEY SAY IN SHOW BUSINESS, TIME IS MONEY!

AND ACCORDING TO OUR BUDGET, EVERY MINUTE WE WASTE IS LIKE THIRTY-TWO CENTS DOWN THE DRAINS, OKAY!

Kermit called for lunch and we all took a well-deserved break.

"Oh, Kermie, dear," trilled Miss Piggy as she entered in her Becky Lorraine camp-counselor outfit. "I just wanted to inform you that tomorrow *moi* will take this production to a new level with a musical and stunt number the likes of which have never been heard nor seen. Gonzo has been training me in the ways of the performance artiste."

"That's great, Piggy," said Kermit, "but you really don't have to do a dangerous stunt. You're memorable and exciting and talented just the way you are."

"You really mean it, Kermie?"

"Sure I do. Just because Sofi is younger and more dexterous doesn't make your classical, old-fashioned entertainment showmanship any less important to the movie."

"Old-fashioned!" bellowed Piggy. "Dexterous! Why, you!!! Hiiiiii-yaaaaaaa!"

I have to admit, I was kind of jazzed about Piggy doing a stunt. Of course, I *am* partial to stunt/music hybrids. I just hoped Gonzo wasn't devoting too much of his time to Piggy's number and ignoring our own big musical stunt for the grand finale.

During lunch, I snuck off with Curtis to the pay phone outside the camp's head office. I wanted to see if I could get in touch with Pasquale and talk him into joining us. With so many dangerous stunts coming up, his expertise was gonna be badly needed.

YOU'VE REACHED THE VOICE MAIL OF PASQUALE. PLEASE LEAVE A MESSAGE AFTER THE TONE, UNLESS YOU'RE A FORMER BEST FRIEND CALLING WITH A FUTILE ATTEMPT TO GET ME TO COME OUT TO A RUN-DOWN SUMMER CAMP AND HELP MAKE SURE SOME CRAZY STUNT DOESN'T GO HORRIBLY WRONG IN A TV MOVIE ABOUT ITCH MEDICATION.

I hung up the phone and sighed. "Well, Curtis, I've really done it. Looks like Pasquale might never speak to me again."

"Don't worry, Danvers," came a voice from behind us. "You still got me, old buddy."

I looked back to see Beebus, cracking his knuckles and grinning from ear to ear. I couldn't help but notice there was no one else around. He had us cornered.

"Uh...hi there, Beebus," I said, trembling. I handed

him the phone. "You need to use the phone? Maybe to call your folks back home at the Block City Zoo reptile exhibit?"

"Very funny. Hardy har har!" He snorted. "Actually, I came 'cause it's lunchtime, and I thought I'd deliver your order personally—one knuckle sandwich with a side of fresh wedgie."

Suddenly, Curtis jumped in between us in his Side Dish outfit and squeaked loudly.

"Awww, look! Your little rat friend is here to protect you. He should really pick on someone his own size." Beebus blew on Curtis like he was blowing out a birthday candle. Curtis rolled away like a tumbleweed. "And now it's your turn!" Beebus lumbered toward me like Frankenstein.

"Uh, yeah." I gulped. "Everything's okay, Kermit. Beebus and I are, uh, Method actors, and we wanna get our scenes just right before we get in front of the camera." Even if Pasquale wasn't speaking to me, I wouldn't throw my friend under the bus with Beebus. I couldn't let him make good on his threat to torture Pasquale on a daily basis.

"Oh, good!" Kermit said as Beebus walked away. Then Kermit announced, "Okay, lunch break is over! Everyone meet down by the old duck pond!"

"The old duck pond?" I shouted. That was where we were going to shoot my big love-song serenade scene with Sofi! Suddenly, I was more nervous than I had been when Beebus's fist was inches from my face.

"How do I look, Curtis?" I said, straightening my hair and breathing into my hand to check my breath—I had snuck some peanut butter and celery sticks in between takes. Curtis almost passed out when he caught a whiff, but then he gave me a spray of breath freshener and we were off.

On a grassy hill by the old duck pond, the crew had laid down a picnic blanket and basket, and my guitar was nestled in the grass. Kermit plopped me down on the blanket and called out, "Okay! All we need is Sofi, and we're ready to shoot!"

To my utter disappointment, Sofi came riding up to the pond on a bike with Kip!

"Sorry I'm late!" Sofi beamed. "Kip was just demonstrating how his hair is impervious to high-speed wind."

TOTALLY. WE WERE GOING, LIKE, FIFTEEN MILES PER HOUR. NOT ONE FOLLICLE WAS DISPLACED, YO. I CREDIT THIS ROOFING-TAR- RIGID-GRIP HAIR GEL.

I had to roll my eyes. "Big whoop."

"That's very impressive, Kip," said Kermit. "But we've got to film Sofi's big picnic scene with Danvers before we run out of sunlight."

"Totes!" Sofi said, getting off the bike and running through the grass toward me.

"Halt!" cried Sam Eagle, as if he were stopping traffic. "Where are your shoes, young lady?!"

Sofi looked down at her bare feet—her beautiful, perfect feet...Sorry! I got distracted there. Sofi looked down at her feet and said, "I left my flip-flops back at the cabin."

Sam plucked a fuzzy little barbed round thing out of the grass.

"I guess I'd better go get my shoes," said Sofi.

Kip stepped up. "Nonsense, yo. I'll just carry you over to the blanket."

"How sweet," said Sofi.

Oh, no, he wouldn't. "*I will clear you a path, madame!*" I shouted.

"Thanks, Danvers!" said Sofi. "How chivalrous!"

I leaned over and whispered to Curtis, "You hear that, Curtis? She called me chivalrous." I wasn't sure what it meant, but it made me happy.

Kip looked irked, and I couldn't help but give him a *Take that!* look.

"That was great, Danvers!" shouted Kermit. "Let's do it again with the cameras rolling. It would be perfect for the scene."

"Uh…okay. I guess we can do it again," I said.

Unfortunately, it took eight more takes to get it perfect. I was starting to feel like a walking pincushion.

After Hockney and Fozzie helped me get the burrs off my face, we were ready to shoot the scene where I sing Sofi a romantic weather-related love song. I had written one especially for the movie.

"Action!" cried Kermit, and the cameras rolled. I picked up my guitar and said in my most suave, smoothest voice, "This song's called 'My Heat Index Is Risin', Girl.'" I strummed the strings and sang, "Baby girl, yo…"

Suddenly, a loud metallic *screeeeeeech* pierced our eardrums and the trees next to us split apart!

A giant robot insect attacked us right in the middle of my beautiful lyrics. Sofi fell back on the grass and the bug hovered over her, its steel claws clamping!

Now was my chance to prove I was a superhero, ready to protect a damsel in distress at any moment. I jumped in front of Sofi and shouted, "Back, you galvanized grasshopper! Don't worry, Sofi! DareDanvers will protect you!"

But Sofi had already jumped up and was striking an open-fist ninja flying-squirrel stance, ready to kick some metal bug butt.

"Was this in the script?" asked Fozzie.

"No, but keep filming. This will save us a fortune on special effects," said Rizzo.

"Cut! Cut! Cut!" yelled a high-pitched, familiar voice, and the robot bug came to a stop. Then something even scarier emerged from the woods.

THIS IS A LIVE FILM SHOOT, PEOPLE! I AM TWYING TO ACT! WAIT A MINUTE! WHAT ARE YOU DOING ON MY SET, BIG BWUDDA?

"Your film set?" I screamed. "This is our set! We're shooting our *Camp Muppet* special here."

"Oh, *contwaire!* We have a permit issued by the Forest Dwellers Association, including the woodchucks. You are interrupting the important scene where I, Penny Pwimwose, and my Fluffleberry fwiends lead the childwen away fwom the Insecta-dwoids."

Fozzie walked up and touched the metal bug. "You mean this is just a special effect? Impressive!"

"This is a state-of-the-art, wemote-contwolled, animatwonic Insectadwoid designed by the best special-effects men in the business," Chloe informed us. "Now, I'm gonna have to ask you all to step aside. We have thwee more scenes to shoot, and we are wapidly approaching my naptime!"

"Sorry, guys," said Kermit. "We can just move over to the koi pond."

"Those koi may not like that," said Pepe. "I hear they are very shy, okay."

"Eetsa all right!" said a voice in a very Italian accent. It was Mondo Gilamonstro, the famous Italian lizard director behind my failed reality show. "Theez are old friends!"

HOW'S IT GOIN', MONDO? LONG TIME NO SEE!

FANTISTICO! THEES FLUFFLEBERRY MOVIE IS GONNA BE DE BEST FILM OF-A MY CAREER. EVEN BETTER THAN *PYGMY PLATYPUSES OF DE CARIBBEAN!*

"You always have to spoil whatever I'm doing, don't you?" I fumed at Chloe.

"You say spoil, I say enhance." Chloe grinned. "Now, just stay out of our way, big bwudda. I won't let your amateur pwoduction interfere with the making of important art. *Adieu!*" She took her film crew and Insectadroid and disappeared into the brush.

"Wow! Your sister's fierce!" said Sofi.

"Like a hyena," I said, frowning.

"Thanks for trying to be all knight-in-shining-armor back there," she added. "Even if the threat was just a special effect."

"You mean it?" I perked up.

"Totes!"

Kip stepped in. "I was totally ready to lay some phat martial-arts maneuvers on that mechabeast, yo."

"Sure you were, yo," I snapped. It felt kinda good to one-up Kip—I cannot lie.

"Hey, Kermit!" shouted Rizzo. "Some folks from the Forest Dwellers Association want to talk to you about filming in the woods."

That night we gathered around the

campfire after an exhausting day of making movie magic. It was really like being at an actual summer camp.

There were campfire songs.

Janice strummed her guitar.

While Animal played the drums.

Pepe told some spooky campfire stories.

We also enjoyed some good ol' fashioned roasted marshmallows.

And, of course, Robo-Beaker dispensed the traditional campfire nacho cheese sauce.

As we enjoyed the fire and looked up at the twinkling stars, Sofi sat right in between me and Kip, which was kinda making me crazy. She was giving Curtis some attention as he warmed his fuzzy belly by the fire.

"It's official—you've got the cutest little rat in the world, Danvers," Sofi said, smiling.

"Thanks, toots!" said Rizzo. "But Danvers doesn't own me. This here rat belongs to no one. I'm a loner, a rebel, a—"

"I was talking about Curtis," Sofi cut him off.

I turned three shades of red at Sofi's compliment. Little did she know that I had bribed Curtis an hour earlier.

Kip was squirming. I could tell he was getting jealous. "I used to have the cutest little hamster you ever did see, yo," he said with a sniffle. "His name was Bosley and we went everywhere together. That is, until that fateful day at the Siberian tiger exhibit."

"Awww, you poor thing," Sofi consoled him.

Kip was practically begging for sympathy just to win Sofi's heart. How despicable! It was clear I was going to have to pull out the big guns.

"Did I ever tell you the story about my puppy, Gertie, and the tragic runaway-leaf-blower incident?" I started. But that's all I got out. My tale was cut short by the sound of a freaky, bone-chilling howl and a glowing green light on the horizon.

"What was that?" Miss Piggy cried, clutching Kermit.

"Probably just the deadwood tree possessed by the killer gnomes again," said Sam. "Nothing to be afraid of, I assure you."

The green light appeared off in the distance again and a moan echoed through the trees.

"Don't be frightened," Kermit said, comforting Miss Piggy. "I'm sure there is a logical explanation for that ghostly glowing hue and horrific sound."

"Yes," agreed Dr. Honeydew. "It is probably just a natural atmospheric disturbance, like swamp gas, the Northern Lights, or a gigantic solar flare that has created a wave of superheated radiation that will sweep across the galaxy and incinerate our planet in mere nanoseconds—you know, nothing to be afraid of."

OR, IT COULD BE THE GLOWING GREEN GIBLET OF . . . BIG CHICKEN!

"Gonzo," Kermit groaned. "Please don't tell me you're going to scare everyone with more stories about Big Chicken."

"No, nothing too scary," answered Gonzo. "Only that Big Chicken roams the woods at night, lighting her way with her giblet in search of hen scratch. Oh—and if she can't find hen scratch, she sometimes will settle for the pinkie toes of young boys and girls."

Thank goodness Kip and I had Sofi close by, because there was some serious petrified clutching going on.

Something suddenly dawned on me. That glowing green light looked strangely similar to the light I witnessed during my transformation.

I bolted up and said, "Does anybody have the time?"

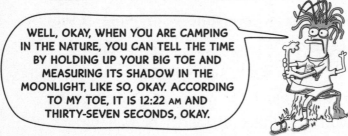

I was stunned. "Twelve twenty-two AM? Do you know what this means?"

"Yeah!" shouted Waldorf. "We should be in bed!"

"That's the same time I transformed into a Muppet two books and 183 pages ago! Something tells me that glowing light might have had something to do with my Muppetmorphosis."

Dr. Honeydew seemed doubtful. "I suppose it is a possibility, but it is highly unlikely. We are miles away from your apartment."

"Still, we have to find the source of that light," I said. "Side Dish, set your camera to night vision." Curtis flipped a switch on his head-mounted camera.

All of a sudden, there was a snap in the woods, like a twig being stepped on!

"What was that, yo?" Kip trembled.

"Big Chicken approaches!" Gonzo said, pulling out a bottle and spraying his neck with a fine mist.

"Why are you putting on cologne?" asked Piggy.

HOW OFTEN DO YOU GET TO MEET A NINE-FOOT CHICKEN? I WANNA MAKE A GOOD IMPRESSION.

HMPH!

I slowly crept toward the brush where I'd heard the twig snap, Curtis on my shoulder.

"Be careful, Danvers," squeaked Sofi.

That's when a giant, monstrous, feathered beast burst out of the trees, screaming ...

I fell back, almost having a heart attack as the rest of the group screeched. Piggy fell off her log, Rizzo dropped his s'mores, and Pepe shed his exoskeleton!

AY CARUMBA! I JUST MOLTED MYSELF!

The giant chicken chased me around the fire three times before I noticed that it was wearing a T-shirt that read PUT THA PEDAL TO THA METAL on it.

"Wait a minute!" I stopped and stood up to the chicken. "That's the same shirt Beebus wears!"

Big Chicken's terrifying roars turned into annoying laughter. The bloated, feathery behemoth reached up and pulled away the chicken mask, revealing his true identity.

Kermit and Fozzie had to hold the karate-chopping Miss Piggy back from Beebus.

"I should have known it was just you being jerky," I said.

"I was just having a little fun," Beebus said, shrugging.

Kermit stood up and calmed everyone down. "It's okay, folks. It was just a joke. Touché, Beebus! You really got us. Now, why don't we all turn in? It's really late and we've got a full day tomorrow."

As Kip and I headed off to our cabin, I caught a glimpse of the green flash on the horizon again—just for a split second. Then it was gone.

"Did you see that?" I asked Kip.

"What, yo?"

"I saw the flash again."

"Dude, it was probably just Beebus playing more tricks. Don't let that big nitwit get to you, yo."

But Beebus was tromping off to his cabin, his flashlight sticking out of his back pocket. There was no way he could have created that flash.

Something was out there.

The next morning it was time to shoot Miss Piggy's big musical wakeboarding number. It seems you just can't make a Muppet production without a huge song-and-dance scene with Miss Piggy—literally. If you try, she'll give you one heck of a karate chop.

First we had to decide where to shoot it. Camp Pain is surrounded by all sorts of bodies of water. There's Lake Imasoe a few hundred yards to the north—famous for the beautiful Imasoe Shore. Then there's the Krymea River, which flows right through the camp. To the west there's the Pew-Jet Sound sewage treatment center, home to five thousand endangered species of gastrointestinal parasites.

Plus, Camp Pain has its own swimming pool, but I wouldn't suggest swimming in it. I don't think it's seen a pool guy in twenty years.

Piggy had changed the script to *Camp Muppet* so that her character, Becky Lorraine, was an aspiring singer, Coverpig make-up model, and gold medal champion wakeboarder. So for her big musical number she decided to sing "Wake Me, I'm Board" while zipping around the lake, culminating the act with a jaw-dropping jump from a wooden ramp.

The Lake Imasoe boardwalk was hustling and bustling with stunt preparation. Hockney was helping Piggy get onto her wakeboard, Gonzo was poring over the stunt diagrams he had drawn up, and Statler and Waldorf were doing a little fishing off the dock. They were rehearsing for their roles as two old cranky guys who like to fish off the dock, of course.

Kermit was running around, prepping the camera, organizing the extras, and looking really, really worried.

"Hey, Danvers," he said quietly to me, so no one

else would hear, "don't tell anyone, but I'm really, really worried. I'm just not sure we should attempt a stunt without Pasquale here to make sure it goes off smoothly and safely."

I had to agree. I approached Gonzo about it. "Hey, Gonzo. Shouldn't we wait until we can find a suitable safety officer before we launch Miss Piggy off a ramp?"

NEVER FEAR, DANVERS. OUR NEW SAFETY OFFICER IS MAKING ADJUSTMENTS TO THE ENGINE AS WE SPEAK!

Miss Piggy overheard us. "That guy is the safety officer?" she roared. "What happened to the little sickly kid with the forehead?"

"Oh, Pasquale?" I said. "We had a falling-out."

"Don't worry, madame," Gonzo said reassuringly. "Crazy Harry is definitely the best in the business."

OR AT LEAST THE CRAZIEST AND THE HAIRIEST, OKAY.

At last, it was time for the stunt. Rizzo got the camera rolling, Scooter asked for quiet on the set, Gonzo fired up the boat, and Piggy grabbed her tow rope, ready to take off across the water.

"Piggy," Kermit called out, "are you sure you want to do this? You don't have to do dangerous and daring stunts to impress me, you know."

"But of course, Kermie," said Piggy. "How hard can this be? Remember, I did all my own roller-skating stunts in *The Muppets Take Manhattan*, and once I even wore white sandals after Labor Day on the red carpet in Cannes."

"That *is* pretty daring. Okay, then," Kermit whimpered. "Let's do this."

"Action!" yelled Kermit.

"Cut!" Kermit yelled as Gonzo sped off toward the horizon and Piggy sailed off over the clouds. "Oh, dear! Better send out a search party," he told Scooter. "Both air and sea!"

"That would never have happened on my watch," said a familiar voice from behind us. We all turned to see a glorious sight: Pasquale! And he had his safety kit with him.

I ran up to Pasquale, jumping with joy. "I'm so glad you're here! It just hasn't been the same without you!"

"I'm only here because Kermit left me a message saying he was in serious need of a safety officer—nothing more," Pasquale said, looking away from me.

Even though he was still irked with me, I was glad to see my best bud.

Kermit looked at his watch, stressed. "Sheesh! We're losing valuable time. We really have to keep filming. I hope Piggy and Gonzo get back soon."

Scooter ran up. "According to the radar, Piggy is somewhere over the next county!"

Kermit looked perplexed. "We have to shoot something."

I looked at Curtis and nodded. This was my chance to slip into my alternating ego! I darted behind the boathouse for a quick wardrobe change. Then…

Rizzo nodded. "Pepe's actually right. Our contract says we have to have a hopping musical number every five minutes."

"But an action scene would really liven this thing up!" I protested.

Kermit agreed with Rizzo. "Sorry, Danvers. But this just isn't that kind of story. We're trying to tell a tale with some real dramatic heft and emotional resonance."

KERMIT! I JUST ADDED AN EXCITING SEQUENCE WHERE CAMP LEADER HOZEN PILOTS A RAFT MADE OUT OF WHOOPEE CUSHIONS. IT'S CALLED A *GAS*-BOTTOMED BOAT! WOCKA! WOCKA!

I WILL NOT BE A PARTY TO THIS.

I took off my DareDanvers mask, completely bummed. "I understand," I said with a sigh. "But who's gonna do another musical number? It could take hours to find Piggy and Gonzo."

I'D DO IT, BUT I'M ALREADY LATE FOR MY CONTRACTUALLY OBLIGATED FIVE-MONTH HIBERNATION. IT'S RIGHT HERE, LISTED UNDER "BEAR NECESSITIES."

Kermit was losing hope. "We've only got a few more days to shoot this whole production. Someone's just gotta have a song in their heart."

Pasquale looked worried. "Will you two be able to handle all the rollicking song and dance? No offense, but you guys are getting up there a bit."

"Are you kiddin'?" said Waldorf. "We're old-school song-and-dance fellas from way back! We even played Caesar's palace."

"Yep! Tap-dancing in those togas was brutal!" Statler laughed.

Rizzo got the cameras rolling, The Electric Mayhem Band started jammin', Statler and Waldorf jumped into a motorboat—well, more like slowly hobbled into the boat—and Kermit shouted, "Action!"

Go Jump in a Lake!
(sung to the tune of Go Bake a Cake!)

You say you're gettin' bored
with summer camp.
You miss your video games
and your skateboard ramps.
and your suggestion to make—
we've got a suggestion to make—
Go Jump in a Lake!

It may not be as clean
as your swimming pool.
But when you hit that frigid water,
it's pretty cool.
Here's advice you oughta take—
Go Jump in a Lake!

Instead of playing loud music at the talent show,
why dontcha head down to the beach?
Forget that "No swimming" sign—it's just for show.
You can guitar with a gar, or lunch with a leech!

I know your dance moves
are hard to top.
But nothing beats a bongo-bangin'
super belly flop!
The icy depths await—
Go jump in a Lake!

Nevermind the snakes,
I hear the swimming's great!
Go Jump in a Lake!

It's forty-three degrees,
and that's without the breeze!
Go jump in a Lake!

Ignore the snappin' gators!
worry about 'em later!
Go Jump in a Lake!

The musical number ended with a huge splash—literally! For the finale, Statler and Waldorf pulled a sharp turn and drenched everyone on the pier!

Pasquale helped them dock the boat and then wrote up a detailed report analyzing the safety of the stunt. Kermit gave him a hearty pat on the back and said, "It's good to have you on board again, Pasquale!"

We took a break for lunch and I followed Pasquale along the trail next to the lake. I could tell he wanted to be alone, so I hung back a few yards. There was so much I wanted to tell him about—the glowing green mystery light, the legend of Big Chicken—but mostly I wanted to tell him about Sofi.

Finally I couldn't stand it anymore. "Pasquale!" I said, grabbing him and turning him around. "I'm sorry! You're the best friend ever! I can't bear to have you mad at me! I know you need your distance right now, but there's this awesome girl I've got to tell you about! Her name is Sofi! She skateboards. She plays guitar. She writes songs! She—"

"She's in a kayak with Kip," Pasquale said, pointing toward the lake.

I couldn't believe it. Not only was Kip on the lake with the girl of my dreams, he was singing her a cheese-ball song. And not just any cheese-ball song— one of the ones off that awful kiddie album! That's, like, a cheese ball with nuts on it!

"Sorry, dude," Pasquale said as he turned to walk back to camp.

I stood there alone by the water, part depressed, part fuming mad as the two lovebirds rowed around the bend, getting lost in the cattails.

"Maybe I should just let him win," I said, sighing. "There's no way I can compete with that magnitude of smoothness."

I felt a tug at my pants leg and looked down to see Curtis madly trying to get my attention. "Don't tell me," I groaned. "Beebus is behind me again."

"Man, you're good! You know me so well!" Beebus cackled, picking me up by my ankle and dunking my head in the lake over and over. I just let him do it. My waterlogged mind was filled with thoughts about Sofi. I couldn't give her up. I wouldn't! I had to confront Kip and take a stand. Of course, it's hard to take a stand when you're upside down, being used as a human plunger.

Beebus yawned and dropped me in a wet clump on the shore, then tromped on back to camp.

"Side Dish," I called out. Curtis ran up and tickled my ear with his nose whiskers. "Operation Takedown initiated."

Curtis squeaked three times, which translates to "Affirmative," and I pulled myself off the wet grass and started back to my cabin.

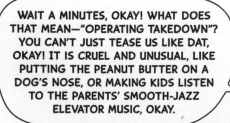

WAIT A MINUTES, OKAY! WHAT DOES THAT MEAN—"OPERATING TAKEDOWN"? YOU CAN'T JUST TEASE US LIKE DAT, OKAY! IT IS CRUEL AND UNUSUAL, LIKE PUTTING THE PEANUT BUTTER ON A DOG'S NOSE, OR MAKING KIDS LISTEN TO THE PARENTS' SMOOTH-JAZZ ELEVATOR MUSIC, OKAY.

In our cabin that night, we made room for Pasquale to plop down his sleeping bag. There was some serious bad mojo in the air. I was irked at Kip for moving in on Sofi, and Pasquale still was standoffish with me over my decision to leave Coldrain.

"The tension in here is palpable," Hockney whined.

"Tell me about it," Gonzo said, sighing. "I'm really in the henhouse with Camilla, too. She's upset that I've been giving Miss Piggy so much attention."

BUT YOU LAUNCHED MISS PIGGY A THOUSAND FEET INTO THE AIR INTO GATOR-INFESTED MARSHLANDS, YO.

YOU'RE RIGHT. HOW COULD I HAVE BEEN SO SELFISH? I LET PIGGY HAVE ALL THE FUN!

"Well, I just wish we could all get along and be happy," Hockney added.

"*Oui!*" Danny agreed.

"I'm totally happy, yo," said Kip. "I've never been so content."

"Why wouldn't you be?" I exploded. "You spent the day kayaking with the most beautiful girl in the world while Beebus was testing me for absorption and buoyancy!"

"I knew it. You're jealous, yo."

"Why did you have to go and ask her out? You already get all the girls' attention in school. It's that hair of yours—it's like a magnet!"

Kip tried to calm me down. "You're right. My hair makes me a girl magnet, but I like Sofi because she is a rocker, yo."

"But Sofi is a skateboarding extreme-stunt lover!" I yelled. "She couldn't be any more right for me."

"If only she were a chicken, she'd be perfect!" added Gonzo.

"Whoa!" said Kip. "This is just like our characters in the movie, yo. We've totally got a love revelry going on here, dude."

"The word is 'rivalry,' dude," I snapped. "And may the best man win!"

Pasquale stayed strangely quiet during our argument. I went to bed irritated. It felt like I was losing both of my best friends. I lay there, trying desperately to get to sleep, but my thoughts were all murky with anger and frustration. After everyone else was snoring peacefully, I sat up, grabbed a scrap of paper and a pen and started scribbling. Then, I snuck over to my duffel bag for a quick wardrobe change.

I slunk out the door and through the quiet, dark campground with Side Dish on my shoulder. I tried to zip from shadow to shadow so no one would spot me. At last, I came upon my destination—Sofi's cabin.

That's when I heard a strange rustling in the bushes. I stopped and scanned the perimeter. It felt like someone was following me, but all was quiet.

I did a ninja roll over to the cabin, which was really dumb because the ground was loaded with grass burrs. Then I pulled out my note, marked Sofi, and started to place it under the door.

That's when the door suddenly opened.

"Maybe we should read it right now!" Beebus chortled, emerging from the shadows. I knew someone had been following me! He snatched my note and read it aloud: "*Dear Sofi, I was wondering if you'd like to have some free trapeze and juggling lessons sometime? Your pal, Danvers.*"

Beebus stuffed the note in my mouth, then lumbered away, laughing.

"That guy's a total bozo," said Sofi nicely. "Don't let him get to you, Danvers."

But I was so embarrassed I took off sprinting back to my room.

Pasquale was waiting outside for me. "You know, you can't let that creep ruin your life. You gotta tell on him."

"So you've been following me, too, huh?" I grumbled. "I thought you weren't talking to me."

"Well, I can't very well let that yeti get away with his behavior."

"Don't worry about Beebus," I said. "I have a plan. Or should I say, DareDanvers has a plan!"

I was just about to reveal my top secret scheme when we heard a *crash* and a ringing sound!

"No, no, no," I said. "Big Chicken is this…oh, I'll explain it later!"

Then we heard another *crash* and saw some lights flickering in Dr. Honeydew's cabin.

"We'd better go check on Dr. Honeydew and Beaker!" I said, adjusting my super goggles. "This could be a job for DareDanvers!"

When we got to Dr. Honeydew and Beaker's cabin, we burst through the door and struck some impressive superhero poses—well, at least Curtis and I did. Pasquale looked kind of embarrassed.

WHAT'S GOING ON IN HERE? WE HEARD A RINGING, FOLLOWED BY A CRASH!

OH, I WAS JUST BAKING SOME COOKIES IN BEAKER'S CONVECTION OVEN WHEN I BURNT MYSELF AND TOSSED THE WHOLE BATCH ONTO THE FLOOR. WHAT A WASTE!

"Yeah," I agreed. "Tossing your cookies is never a pleasant experience."

Pasquale tugged on my cape and said, "We'll just be going now, Dr. Honeydew. Didn't mean to disturb you."

"Oh, no problem at all," said Dr. Honeydew. "As a matter of fact, there was something I wanted to discuss with you. Something quite frightening."

"Oh, boy," groaned Pasquale. "Here we go."

Dr. Honeydew handed me a newspaper. "I want

you to take a look at this old paper and tell me what you see."

THEY'VE GOT COVERTS TENNIS SHOES HALF OFF AT THE FOOT BARN!

"More important, read the headline," said the doc.

"The Baseball Diamond was stolen in England?" I read aloud. "Wait a second! Wasn't that the name of the diamond in *The Great Muppet Caper*?"

"Correct," said Dr. Honeydew. Then he pulled out a big, thick book. "Now, look at the photo of Charles Dickens on the back of this copy of *A Christmas Carol*."

I couldn't believe my eyes. On the back of the cover was a photo of Dickens, except he looked exactly like Gonzo, wearing a top hat and a scarf.

"Didn't Gonzo play Charles Dickens in

The Muppet Christmas Carol?" asked Pasquale.

"Precisely," said Dr. Honeydew. "A fictional diamond theft showing up in a real newspaper. A cinematic portrayal of Dickens making its way onto an actual novel. Some might say it's a coincidence, some might call it curious, and others might claim it's a shameless plug for other Muppet merchandise."

"I told you," I said, "things have been wacky ever since I transformed, starting with Veterinarian's Hospital and the Muppet Theater being in the middle of Block City!"

YES. IT'S ALL, AS FELLOW SCIENTISTS WOULD SAY, "ABSOLUTELY CRAZY-BOBBLES," "COMPLETELY WHACKADIZZLE," AND LET'S NOT FORGET TOTALLY EMPIRICALLY INSANE IN THE MEMBRANE!

DOCTOR, PLEASE. SOME OF OUR READERS MIGHT NOT UNDERSTAND SUCH COMPLEX SCIENTIFIC TERMS!

"So, what are you saying, Doc?" asked Pasquale. "Do you think Danvers's Muppetmorphosis affected more than just Danvers?"

Dr. Honeydew walked to his microscope and motioned us over. "I'm afraid I haven't even shown you my most disturbing discovery. Take a look at this sample I pulled from the water nearby."

I peered into the microscope and adjusted the focus. What I saw was crazy.

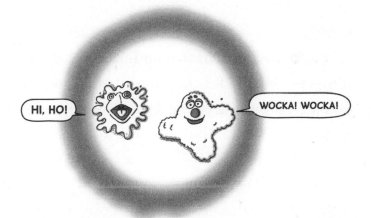

"No way!" I gasped.

"These strange creatures have never been seen in real life before, yet they oddly resemble critters that once showed up in an old *Muppet Show* comedy sketch," said Dr. Honeydew. "Notice their similarities to Kermit and Fozzie. I believe these organisms are also a result of the same phenomenon that caused you to change."

"What does it all mean, Doc?" I asked.

Dr. Honeydew sat down and rubbed his forehead. "I'm not sure, but it is essential that we reverse your Muppetmorphosis, young Danvers. If not for your sake, for the sake of life as we know it. Your transformation created an imbalance, a rift in the universe, and, just like Ivy League Poison Ivy Itch Relief Crème with soothing aloe gel, it is only going to spread."

As Pasquale, Curtis, and I left

Dr. Honeydew's cabin and made our way back across the moonlit grounds, we heard a weird clicking sound. We slowly snuck past the main cabin, where Sam Eagle was cutting some serious Zs, then we tiptoed around the rancid swimming pool, following the strange sounds.

"Halt! Who goes there?" a voice blurted out, seriously testing my heart-attack threshold.

It was Rowlf the Dog, and he was winding something in his paw.

> ROWLF! WHAT ARE YOU DOING OUT HERE THIS LATE? AND WHAT ARE THOSE THINGS YOU'RE WINDING?

> I WAS TOLD WE WERE DONE WITH CLOCK PUNS AND HAD MOVED ON TO ITCH-CREAM HUMOR.

> SAM EAGLE PUT ME ON *WATCH* DETAIL. LUCKILY, MY SHIFT IS *WINDING* DOWN.

"Why do we need a night watchman?" I asked. "Aside from the snakes, gators, rank swimming-pool water, razor-sharp grass burrs, rusty nails, spooky deadwood trees, broken glass, sewage plant, and resident bully, this camp seems pretty safe to me."

"Orders from Sam Eagle," said Rowlf. "I think he got a little spooked by all that Big Chicken talk. It's not often a chicken gives an eagle goose bumps. That can be confusing to a bird. Kinda like when I get the urge to take a catnap."

Pasquale looked perplexed. "I still don't know what all this Big Chicken talk is about."

So I explained the legend of the behemoth bird— her appetite for hen scratch, the giant chicken prints she leaves behind, and the glowing green giblet.

"Kinda like that glowing green light over there," said Rowlf, pointing to the horizon.

Sure enough, a green flash flickered for a few seconds about a hundred yards away.

"We should go check it out," I said.

"Well, we're gonna go investigate," I announced. "I suspect that light has nothing to do with abnormally large chickens, but it may be the key to why I am a Muppet."

"Then I guess I'm coming with you to provide protection," said Rowlf. "I may not be a vicious guard dog, but I'll do in a pinch!"

"Let me guess," said Pasquale. "Because you're part Doberman *pinsc*her."

"You learn quick," Rowlf said, chuckling. "Now, any second my replacement should be here to take over."

HOLA, MY FRIENDS, OKAY. I AM HERE TO STAND GUARDS. I WARN YOU, I AM VERY SLEEPY, SO SOMEBODY BETTER RELIEVE ME SOON, OKAY.

SORRY, PRAWN. YOU'RE THE LAST SHIFT OF THE NIGHT. THERE WON'T BE ANYONE RELIEVING YOU.

THEN I GUESS I WILL HAVE TO RELIEVE MYSELF, OKAY.

We started off into the dark woods with Rowlf as our guide. Curtis flipped his camera to night vision and I changed my pink doughnut goggles to the more camouflaged chocolate variety.

"Be careful, okay!" Pepe called out. "Say hi to the *pollo grande* for me!"

The woods were creepy and kinda weird. In every dark nook and cranny I could see glimmering eyes staring at us. Whimpers and howls filled the air, and I could have sworn I heard the sound of...panting?

I pulled out my bedazzled DareDanvers pocket flashlight and shined it into the woods. I couldn't believe my eyes—the trees were full of poodles, schnauzers, Afghans, Chihuahuas, and every other type of pooch!

Pasquale leaned in to me and said, "This must be part of what Dr. Honeydew was talking about. The whole world is starting to come unhinged."

That's when we saw the green light again. This time it looked like it was only a few yards away. A low rumble filled the air, the ground started to shake, and the light got closer and brighter. "Stay behind me," I said as I walked toward the glow. "Something horrifying could be lurking behind that light."

What lurked behind that light was more horrifying than I could ever have imagined.

I couldn't believe it. The brat was back. "Aren't you done with that dumb Fluffleberry movie yet?" I griped.

"Hardly!" said Chloe. "This is a big-budget Holly-wood pwoduction! We'll be shooting 'til the end of the week, then weshooting for the next thwee months. Then there are test scweenings and focus gwoups, and of course we have to manufacture the new Chloe: Savior of the Fluffleberries action figure. Sometimes I envy you and your quaint, amateur pwoject."

"Quaint? Amateur?" I laughed. "I'll have you know *Camp Muppet* is chock-full of hard-hitting dialogue."

"Exciting special effects."

"Groundbreaking stuntwork."

226

"And a cast of thousands."

Rowlf came up to us and said, "Looks like the green glow was just from the cannon on top of their tank."

"You mean the Quadra-3000 Wapid-Load Pulse Laser Cannon with infrared sighting and gyrating spectra turbines?" Chloe corrected him.

"Uh...yeah," said Rowlf.

I pulled Chloe aside while her film crew took a break. "So, have you talked to Mom and Dad? I've been feeling a little guilty—both of us leaving them all alone and everything."

"No, I haven't talked to them," Chloe said, dropping her cutesy accent. (Notice how she only drops it when she's speaking to me privately because she knows I'm onto her little-miss-innocent-angel shtick.)

Chloe pulled out a postcard and said, "But they did send me this weird picture postcard of them river-rafting in the Himalayas."

"That's really strange," I said. "Why would they send us a Mount Everest postcard?"

Chloe shook her head. "They're so cute. Pretending to be having fun so we won't worry about them."

"Yeah," I agreed. "They must be miserably bored."

Pasquale and I stayed up way too late, and the next morning, I did not want to crawl out of that sleeping bag. Luckily, Sam Eagle, being the military man he was, had an effective way of waking us up.

RISE AND SHINE, FUTURE DILIGENT AND PRODUCTIVE CITIZENS OF BLOCK CITY! EVERYONE CONVENE AT BREAKFAST IN TEN MINUTES! SWEDISH CHEF HAS PROMISED SOMETHING THAT'S ACTUALLY EDIBLE THIS MORNING.

I was just about to get up when, suddenly, Beebus appeared, standing over me. "You heard him—up and at 'em, Danvers!"

Beebus zipped me into my sleeping bag completely, then picked the whole thing up and started twirling me above his head like a lasso.

I WONDER HOW FAR I CAN THROW YOU, MUPPET BOY? MY RECORD IS THIRTY FEET, BUT THAT WAS USING AN UNDERNOURISHED KINDERGARTNER.

Beebus released me and I'm proud to say I only flew about ten feet. Of course, that's because the cabin wall kept me from going any farther.

Beebus laughed maniacally on his way out the door, while Pasquale and Kip helped me up.

"Dude, yo," said Kip. "I'm reporting that Cro-Magnon to Kermit. I don't care what you say, yo."

"I have to concur," Pasquale added. "This treatment is unacceptable."

"I told you guys not to worry," I said, putting on my superhero doughnut mask. "DareDanvers is on the case."

Kermit ran up to the front of the eating area and said, "Hi-ho, early risers! Today, I thought we'd do something kind of fun. So just as soon as you finish eating your breakfast, come on up front."

IF WE EAT ANY MORE OF THIS BREAKFAST, WE *WILL* BE FINISHED! HA HA!

After breakfast, everyone gathered in front of a big screen Kermit had set up for us.

"Now," Kermit started. "In big Hollywood productions, we like to do something special called 'screening the dailies.'"

AH, YES, THE DAILY SPECIAL. I HOPE IT IS NOT SEAFOOD SURPRISE, OKAY!

"No, no," said Kermit. "'Screening the dailies.' That's where we watch some of the scenes from the movie that we've already shot. It's a way to check our progress, compliment the actors, see what we can do to make it better...."

"And put everyone to sleep!" shouted Waldorf.

Screening the dailies was fun. First we watched Piggy's big stunt gone wrong, which got a big reaction from the crowd.

Piggy said, "Why does everyone think it's so funny when I launch into the clouds?"

Fozzie replied, "Don't worry. We are laughing at you, not with you. Wait…maybe I said that wrong."

Then we watched the scene where I sang to Sofi at the picnic. "Good job, you two!" Kermit praised us.

"Bravo!" I shouted, much to Kip's annoyance. Sofi turned red with embarrassment.

After the applause died down, I stood up to make a special announcement. "I'd like to personally introduce the next video. It features the person who I feel has given the most believable, realistic performance in *Camp Muppet* so far. Ladies and gentlemen, I give you Beebus."

"Awww, shucks," said Beebus, pretending to be bashful.

"Side Dish!" I yelled. "Initiate Operation Take-down!"

Curtis ran up to the big screen and plugged his tail into the USB slot on the side. A grainy video image popped up on the screen.

"Hey, it's Beebus!" shouted Rizzo. "This doesn't look like a scene from our script, though."

Beebus got a horrified look on his face.

"Beebus," said Gonzo, "why are you dangling Danvers above the lake? And why are you shoving melted marshmallows down his shorts?"

And I wasn't kidding. Every awful thing Beebus had done to me during the week played out for the whole room to see: swirlies, practical jokes, wedgies, insults, the entire spectrum of nitwittery!

"Young man, this is appalling!" huffed Sam Eagle.

"Beebus," said Kermit, "can you explain these videos?"

"We were just practicing our upcoming scenes," said Beebus, giving me the evil eye. "Isn't that right, Danvers?"

"Is this true?" Kermit asked me.

"Not really," I said.

"Okay! Okay!" Beebus groaned. "So I was just having a little fun. Big whoop!"

"Sheesh," said Kermit. "That's a strange idea of fun."

Piggy let out a steady growl, a sure sign of that karate chop was brewing.

Sam Eagle stood up. "This cannot be allowed to stand! It is a blatant violation of Camp Pain ethics!"

"Yeah," agreed Fozzie. "Kermit, I think you'll have to let Beebus go. I'd do it, but I'm not so good with confrontation."

Kermit looked bummed. "I've never had to fire somebody before. It's really difficult."

"That does it," said Kermit. "Beebus, I hate to have to do this, but I don't think you can be in our movie."

"But you can't replace me! Who's gonna play the bully?" Beebus cried.

Kermit opened the door for him. "You know

what? We don't have room in our cast for a bully."

Beebus walked out, then turned back to us, shouting, "I'll get you for this, DareDanvers! Just wait 'til we get back to—" Miss Piggy shut the door in his face before he could finish.

HMPH! DON'T LET THE DOOR HIT YOU ON THE WAY OUT, BUSTER!

SLAM!

"Way to go, DareDanvers!" Sofi shouted, and everyone in the room clapped. "And Side Dish, too!" Curtis took a much-deserved bow.

Pasquale patted me on the back. "You handled that admirably. I guess I was wrong to think you'd just let that bruiser walk all over you."

"I was just biding my time."

Kermit put a hand on my shoulder. "You should have told us sooner, Danvers."

"I know, Kermit," I said. "I was just worried no one would believe me without hard evidence. And he promised to take it out on Pasquale if I ratted on him, too."

"Don't worry about me," Pasquale scoffed. "I can handle myself. But maybe I should look into hiring a bodyguard."

"Danvers, I'll always believe you and stick up for you," Kermit said. "And if we had the budget for it, I would burst into song right now."

The last few days of the shoot

were running smoothly and efficiently, and they were a lot more fun without the fear of being dangled above a sewage treatment pond hanging over me. But Beebus continued to haunt the production. Instead of going home, the big lug was lurking around in the woods and trying to sabotage everything.

First he hid firecrackers in the marshmallows, making for some explosive s'mores.

Then he bombarded our cabin with rotten eggs.

He committed disgusting acts of vandalism.

And he was constantly trying to scare us by pretending to be Big Chicken.

But we just ignored Beebus and went on with the shoot. We were far too busy filming to put up with his nonsense, anyway.

On Friday, we were just hours away from shooting the finale. Gonzo was putting the finishing touches on the huge stunt that would go along with our song, and Kip was slathering his hair with the strongest gel he had. Suddenly, Rizzo and Fozzie burst in, waving their scripts.

"Hold the phones and stop the presses!" yelled Rizzo.

"We have some last-minute script changes!" added Fozzie.

Rizzo opened up the new script. "In the new ending, Sofi's character, Lana, is such an incredible song-writing talent that she forms a female supergroup led by none other than Miss Piggy."

"I wonder who really came up with that idea?" whispered Pasquale.

"That sounds like a good twist to me," I said. "Sofi deserves the spotlight."

"But that's not all!" said Fozzie. "The new group is so good, the only way to beat them is for Mon Swoon and Emo Shun to join forces as Mon Emo Shun Swoon, or M.E.S.S., just to compete with her. In the finale, they perform the contractually required megahit 'Girl, Don't Be Rash' on a steamboat while Gonzo does a stunt overhead."

Pasquale looked confused. "How were the two bands combined into M.E.S.S. in the original script?"

"Dr. Honeydew was going to throw us into his Twice-Baked Transportater and fuse us into one," I explained. "But due to budget constraints, his scene was cut."

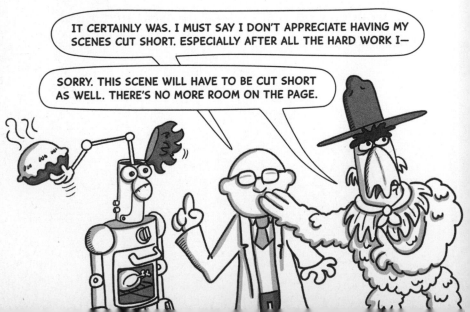

IT CERTAINLY WAS. I MUST SAY I DON'T APPRECIATE HAVING MY SCENES CUT SHORT. ESPECIALLY AFTER ALL THE HARD WORK I—

SORRY. THIS SCENE WILL HAVE TO BE CUT SHORT AS WELL. THERE'S NO MORE ROOM ON THE PAGE.

We were all set to shoot the big Battle of the Bands spectacular on a humongous paddleboat anchored alongside the camp on the Krymea River. There was a stage set up on the top deck of the boat and Kermit was getting the film crew into place while Dr. Teeth rehearsed with the band.

Kip and I were practicing our big song on the shore when Gonzo walked up, decked out in sparkly green long johns.

FEAST YOUR EYES!

"Greetings, fellow stuntmonger," he said. "At long last, I am ready to disclose the details of my final stunt. Wait—that didn't come out right. What I meant to say was, I'm ready to disclose the details of my stunt finale.

"At the emotional apex of the song," he continued, drawing a diagram in the mud with a stick, "I shall zip-line on this steel cable running between this tall peak onshore and the riverboat, at a speed of over one hundred miles per hour, feetfirst, into this pair of tight-fitting sequined disco pants, then perform a traditional Peruvian Kachampa dance on the roof of the boat!"

"As your safety officer, I have to strongly advise against this," warned Pasquale. "It's incredibly risky."

"You're right," said Gonzo. "It's far too early in the year for sequined disco pants. I better go with feathered cha-cha pants instead! Thanks, Pasquale! It's great to have you back!"

I loved it. "Sounds awesome to me, Gonzo!"

Suddenly, Kermit called for everyone to get on board. "Places, everybody! Let's get this show on the road...er, uh, river! First up is Lana and her group, Pry Ora Tee."

"Knock 'em dead!" I gushed to Sofi.

"Yeah, break a leg, yo," said Kip. "Not literally. Just fugitively."

"It's figuratively, yo," I sassed.

Then I got up the nerve to do something I had been dying to do for ages. No, not try hot fudge on a double cheeseburger—I asked Sofi on a real date. "I was wondering," I said to her, "if, after the filming is done, you might wanna take me up on those trapeze lessons or maybe watch some *Muppet Show* episodes on video, or—"

Kip butted in. "Actually, I was wondering if after we're done here, I could take you to a fly concert or a skateboard park or—"

"You guys totes just need to concentrate on your jam!" Sofi giggled, rushing to the stage.

Suddenly, the loud blaring of a foghorn rattled everyone's nerves. I ran to the side of the boat to see a gigantic, futuristic battleship sailing past us. It was about five times as big as Dr. Teeth's riverboat, covered in battle cannons, and looked like it came from the twenty-fifth century.

"She always has to one-up me," I grumbled to Pasquale.

"Actually, I think she just ten-upped you." He smiled as we watched the huge cruiser sail down-river.

After the boat had passed, Sofi's group and the camera crew got into place. It was time to get started!

MISS PIGGY GETS JIGGY, TAKE ONE. OKAY!

Kermit ran up onstage and announced, "Ladies and gentlemen, patrons and matrons and bears wearing aprons—let's give a big hand to our first group in the Battle of the Bands, that bevy of lovely ladies, Miss Piggy, Lana, Janice, and Camilla, also known as Pry Ora Tee! Yaaaaay!!!"

THIS SONG'S CALLED "ALL THE SASSY LADIES." COME ON—LET'S SING IT, GIRLS!

They were so amazingly good. The song Sofi wrote was perfect and, of course, Miss Piggy was a force to be reckoned with.

"Fozzie," I said, "I think you're gonna have to change the script again. Lana's group just has to beat us in the competition. Otherwise it won't be realistic."

"Miss Piggy already made that change," Fozzie pointed out. "She was quite persuasive."

"That's cool," said Kip. "Now we can just go out there and have fun, yo."

M.E.S.S. IS DUE ONSTAGE IN FIVE SECONDS! WAIT A MINUTE! THAT MEANS *I'M DUE ONSTAGE IN FIVE SECONDS*! I BETTER PUT ON MY DANCING SHOES!

It was time for our big final number. We took our places on the deck of the riverboat. Kip gave me the thumbs-up signal. Fozzie, Scooter, Danny, and Cody were ready to hit some serious dance grooves. Animal was poised with his sticks at his drumset. And Gonzo was at the top of the hill across the river, securely attached to his zip-line, which led to a spot on the stage beside me, where Pasquale was holding his feathered pants.

Then the cameras rolled! The lights went up! The music blasted! Kermit ran up and said, "Let's throw your hands, wings, fins, and flippers in the air for our challengers, the ultimate boy band, M.E.S.S.! Yaaaaay!"

The whole boat was hopping with kids dancing to our song. We may not have jammed as hard as Sofi and Piggy's group, but that river was rockin'.

I looked out at the crowd of kids, and I have to say my heart swelled when I saw Sofi looking our way and tapping her foot.

After our big number, we had one more scene to film—Kermit announcing the winner. "Woweee!" Kermit cried, bringing out a huge trophy. "Both numbers were fantastic and deserve a big round of applause! But, unfortunately, we can only name one as Camp Muppet champion, and that band is...Lana and the sassy ladies of Pry Ora Tee! Yaaaaay!"

"Cut!" yelled Kermit. "That's a wrap, folks! You all did a marvelous job! Give yourselves a big hand!"

And that was that. The movie shoot was all done. The hardest week of work I've ever endured was at an end and it felt good. Curtis and I celebrated with some Cheezy-Qs.

Hold your horses, guys! I was just getting to that. How's this?

Suddenly, a loud, piercing scream shattered our celebration. We all looked downriver. There were flashes of light like explosions and a horrific metallic screech like the sound of three hundred forks being scraped on a chalkboard.

"**W**hat was that scream?" asked Miss Piggy.

"Only one thing could produce such a high-pitched eardrum assault," I said ominously. "My little sister!"

More screams echoed across the water.

"It's coming from downriver!" I cried. "Let's go! Dr. Teeth, full steam ahead!"

Dr. Teeth laughed. "Steam? Ha! Steam is for mixed vegetables, my fine fellow! This boat's had some modulations and modifications, if you catch my drift. It runs on rock and roll!"

"Rock and roll?" said Pasquale.

EXACTALUTELY! THE HARDER THE ELECTRIC MAYHEM ROCKS, THE SOONER WE DOCK! NOW PULL UP THE ANCHOR AND HOLD ON TIGHT. BANDMATES—LET'S ROCK THE BOAT!

I couldn't believe it. There was a whole band set up in the engine room. The Electric Mayhem Band started playing some heavy-duty tunage, which revved up the boat's engines. We were on our way!

Pasquale and I ran to the stern of the boat, where everyone was gathered. Our riverboat barreled downstream toward the commotion.

"Look! Up ahead!" cried Sofi. "It's that ship that passed us earlier with your sister on it!"

As Dr. Teeth pulled our boat up alongside the battle cruiser, I could see Chloe and the rest of the crew battling the Insectadroids on board.

"They're just filming a scene!" I scoffed. "We zoomed all the way over here for nothing. We better get out of their shot before my sister yells at us again!"

"I don't think this is make-believe," whimpered Fozzie.

"Why's that?" I asked.

"Because the bugs just threw the director overboard!"

We looked up to see a wayward lizard hurtling toward us! We jumped aside just in time for Mondo to land on the deck with a *fwump*!

THEES CAST IS A MORE DIFFICULT THAN *THE HOSTILE HOUSEWIVES OF NEW HAMPSHIRE*!

I ran up to Mondo and helped him sit up. "What happened over there, Mondo?"

"It was a-horrible!" he said, trembling. "The Insectadroids! They go—how you say—haywired! They attack us! They a-humiliate me! They throw me over the board! Other than that, it was a good time!"

Kermit looked perplexed. "Why would the special-effects robots from their movie start revolting?"

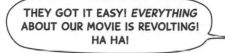

THEY GOT IT EASY! *EVERYTHING* ABOUT OUR MOVIE IS REVOLTING! HA HA!

"There's a-one more thing!" cried Mondo.

"Thata ship has no *capitano*! De bugs throwa him into the river!"

"We've gotta get everyone off that ship and onto this boat!" I yelled, peering over the edge. We were moving really fast. The current seemed to be getting stronger and stronger.

"But how, yo?" asked Kip.

STEP ASIDE! IT'S TIME WE PUT MY ZIP LINE AND CHA-CHA PANTS TO GOOD USE!

Gonzo twirled the zip-line above his head like a cowboy twirling a rope, and slung it toward the other boat.

Chloe tied off the line, then she and the rest of the crew zip-lined over to our riverboat. Chloe was the last to come over.

Once my little sis was on board, I did the unthinkable—I hugged the wee monster!

"No time for schmaltzy stuff, big bwudda!" Chloe yelled. "You've gotta help my friends the Pipipski twins!" She pointed down at a tiny lifeboat in between the two ships with two little girls in it. They were fending off an Insectadroid with a paddle, and they had a hole in their boat. "The lifeboat is sinking!"

"I've got to get down there!" I cried.

Suddenly I felt something tugging at the back of my pants leg. I turned to see Curtis again. He had my superhero gadget case.

"Curtis! You're a genius!" I yelled, quickly rummaging through the case and grabbing my toilet plunger–grappling hook.

A loud voice came over the riverboat loud-speaker. It was Dr. Teeth, calling from the helm with some rotten news. "This might be an opportune time to introduce one more plot development—we are rapidly approaching Yura Gonner Falls, a spectacular three-hundred-foot drop onto some seriously sharp rocks. Just thought I'd toss that into the mix!"

No wonder the current was getting so strong. We were headed for certain doom at the bottom of the falls!

Pasquale leaned over the railing and shouted down at me, "Get up here, dude! We gotta turn this boat around before it's too late!"

I was just about to start my way up the rope when I heard whimpering from the corner of the lifeboat. I looked over to see something moving and squirming under a heavy blanket. I reached down slowly to rip the blanket away, terrified that it was another Insectadroid. When I pulled the blanket back, I found that it was actually something worse!

"Come on, you big lug!" I roared. "Grab hold of my back and we'll climb up." But as soon as I started up the rope, it snapped. We were too darn heavy.

"What are we gonna do?" cried Beebus.

There weren't many options. I shouted up at the rest of the crew, "You guys might just have to turn around and leave without us! You can't risk everyone just to save us!"

"I don't really like that plan!" said Beebus.

Suddenly, Miss Piggy and Sofi came flying over the railing!

Then they bounced back up to the deck of the boat with us in tow.

Everybody cheered when we made it back on board the riverboat. But we couldn't celebrate for long. The roar of Yura Gonner Falls just ahead was deafening, and we were headed straight for it!

We disconnected the zip-line from the battle cruiser and Dr. Teeth shouted, "Hard to port!" which, for all you non-nautical folks out there, means "Turn left!"

The boat was doing a full-on U-turn in the middle of the raging river, drifting dangerously close to the edge. I had to cling to the railings so that I wouldn't slide overboard.

Curtis clung to my cape, and Pasquale grabbed onto Gonzo's nose.

"I dunno if we're gonna make it, yo!" cried Kip.

But we finally turned completely around! The battle cruiser, along with the rest of the Insectadroids, went right over the falls and disappeared into the mist.

Our riverboat chugged and chugged to get away, but the force of the current was pulling us backward. We weren't going to make it after all!

"Quick!" yelled Kermit. "Drop anchor! Maybe it'll snag on something and keep us from going over!"

KERMIT, I DON'T THINK THIS IS THE KIND OF ANCHOR YOU WERE LOOKING FOR.

ANCHOR

NEWS FLASH!

THIS JUST IN, MORALE IS PLUMMETING AS MUPPET PRODUCTION STRUGGLES TO STAY AFLOAT!

S.O.S

Kermit looked grim. "Well, guys, this could be it."

"Attention, all my fellow musicians!" yelled Dr. Teeth. "Mon Swoon! Emo Shun! Sassy ladies! Get to the engine room, quick! We're in a jam! Or should I say, we need more jam!"

We grabbed our instruments and ran to the engine room.

"I need you cats to pump up the jams and shred some rock and rollage like never before, or else we're gonna hit rock bottom!" yelled Dr. Teeth.

We plugged in our amps and started rockin' with The Electric Mayhem. The boat lurched forward a little bit, but the pull of the waterfall was too much. The boat backed over the falls and we plummeted toward the bottom!

"This is gonna call for some heavy artillery!" Floyd yelled, pulling out an envelope labeled WARNING— DO NOT OPEN WITHOUT WRITTEN CONSENT! He pulled some old sheet music out of the envelope and placed it in front of Animal.

Animal ripped into the craziest drum solo in history, his arms moving at the speed of light. Sparks flew off his cymbals. The paddle-wheel on the steamboat started spinning faster, and the boat climbed up the waterfall back onto the river. The rest of us kicked in and helped power the boat upriver and back to camp.

I don't have to tell you what a relief it was to be back on dry land. Actually, we were back on wet mud, but that was better than hurtling over a waterfall to certain doom.

Onshore, Kermit questioned Beebus. "Did you cause those robot bugs to go haywire?"

Beebus stepped forward and 'fessed up. "I wanted to get a closer look at those Insectadroids, and maybe take one for a test spin. When I finally snuck into the room where they kept 'em, I decided to go ahead and egg them—it's just this thing I like to do. When the egg yolks hit the remote-control circuits, well, the bugs went crazy." Beebus gave me a look of shame. "I still can't figure out why you saved me. I was such a jerk to you."

"Well, Beebus," I said, "I've finally found my Muppet superpower—I always seem to do the right thing, even if it's for the wrong people. Plus, sometimes it just helps to have a removable nose."

"Hey, what are you going to do about that missing nose, anyway?" said Pasquale.

I felt the empty space above my upper lip. "I don't know. I guess now I'll have a lot more room to grow an epic mustache."

I heard a tiny little cough and felt a tug on my jeans.

"Hey!" I shouted. "Curtis must have plucked my schnoz from the jaws of fate at the last second! Thanks, little guy!"

I stuck my soggy nose back on my face and breathed a sigh of relief.

One of the Insectadroids must have hitched a ride on the riverboat! It crawled out of the murky mud onto the shore and started coming for us, its iron jaws snapping.

Swedish Chef tried to fight it with a frying pan, but he was batted away like a Ping-Pong ball.

Lew Zealand hurled one of his boomerang fish at the droid, but it had no effect.

The beast was just about to overtake us. All hope seemed lost.

Suddenly, a loud *klang* got everyone's attention, followed by the sound of a grating robotic "MEEP!"

It was Robo-Beaker! And Chloe was riding on his shoulders. "Hey! Bug bwain!" she yelled at the Insectadroid.

Beaker launched rapid-fire burnt toast, scalding-hot espresso, and freshly whipped cream. The robot giants went head-to-head in a clanging, screeching, scraping clash of the mecha monsters.

Robo-Beaker blinded the beast with some freshly squeezed lemon juice, but the Insectadroid returned with an uppercut to Beaker's aluminum jaw.

"Oh, dear!" said Dr. Dr. Honeydew. "I'm afraid that may have dislocated Beaker's jaw, or even worse, voided his warranty!"

Suddenly, Kip ran up with his emergency hair-gel kit.

LUCKILY I GOT ALL OF THIS ON VIDEO! THIS IS GONNA BE ONE GREAT ACTION MOVIE. OH, WAIT—I FORGOT TO LOAD THE CAMERA! WE'RE GONNA HAVE TO FILM IT AGAIN!

The Insectadroid was…well, let's just say he was feeling a little scattered. Everyone gave Kip and Robo-Beaker a cheer.

"Way to go, guys!" said Gonzo. "You saved the day!"

"I think a wrap party is in order!" announced Kermit.

Pepe ran up with some fresh fruit and shouted, "What do you say we celebrate with some fresh smoothies, okay?"

Pepe connected a glass pitcher to the top of Beaker's head, threw in some mangoes and bananas, and searched for the right button on the back of Beaker's head.

LET'S SEE, OKAY. BLEND, STIR, LIQUIFY, PULVERIZE, NORMAL!

He pressed the NORMAL button and Beaker started to vibrate and meep uncontrollably. There was a huge flash and a puff of smoke. As the smoke cleared, Beaker emerged from it looking like his old self!

"Hey! Beaker is no longer Robo-Beaker!" I cried.

"My, oh, my," said Dr. Honeydew. "Apparently, the answer was right in front of us all along. He is completely back to normal."

WELL, ALMOST NORMAL.

I was kinda bummed, I have to say. I looked down at my felty, wobbly body. "I wish I had a NORMAL button I could just push."

"I don't think that word ever applied to you," said Pasquale. "Nor should it."

That's when Kip and I both noticed Sofi. She was over near the picnic tables, kind of away from the crowd.

"Okay, Sofi," I said, running up to her. "You still haven't given us your answer. Do you wanna do some trapeze stunts and watch some Gonzo videos with me, or do you wanna see some lame-o concert with Kip?"

"Yeah, girl," said Kip. "I gotta know, too. It's tearin' up my heart, yo. What's your decision? Drumroll please!"

"Drumroll?!" shouted Animal before passing out cold.

Sofi smiled and patted both of us on the back. "You dudes are super cool…but I gots to say I'm more into brainpower. This Saturday, Pasquale and I are gonna go build our own battery out of copper wires and a potato."

We looked at Pasquale, dumbfounded. "I don't get it," I said. "How are you such a ladies' man?"

IT'S LIKE FOZZIE SAID: "ALL GOOD STORIES AND PRETZELS SHOULD HAVE A TWIST. WOCKA! WOCKA!"

That night, as we were packing our bags, Pasquale and I were a little glum. I couldn't believe I wasn't going to be joining him at Coldrain the next morning. Instead I'd be turning my education and creative career over to Sam Eagle.

Pasquale pulled something out of his backpack and handed it to me.

"*Math for Dimwits?*" I said, startled.

"You're gonna need it, since I won't be there to help you pass pop quizzes anymore," Pasquale said, grinning.

"I don't know whether to be offended or grateful," I said. "So you're not mad at me about leaving?"

Pasquale sighed. "Not mad. Just sad. But after

watching you having so much fun shooting this movie and performing with M.E.S.S., I've come to realize that Eagle Talon is definitely where you need to be."

"You know," I said as I shoved the book into my bag, "just because we'll be going to different schools doesn't mean you can get out of supervising me being hurled from cannons, launched from catapults, dragged by go-carts, and other forms of extreme torture—I mean, stunts."

"Yeah," Pasquale said, smiling. "But nothing will be more torturous than climbing the rope in Coach Kraft's class or listening to Buttons recite iambic pentameter in English."

Pepe suddenly burst into the room, holding a big box. "*Hola*, my friends! I have your payment for all the hard working you did, okay!"

"All right, yo!" said Kip. "Cash money!"

"Not quite, okay," said Pepe as he opened up the box and revealed the mother lode of Ivy League Poison Ivy Itch Crème.

"We're being paid in itch cream?" I scoffed.

YES! AS THE IVY LEAGUE PEOPLE ALWAYS SAY, "*SPREAD* THE WEALTH!"

GEEZ! I THOUGHT THIS PRODUCTION WAS CHEAP, BUT NOW THEY'RE JUST *RUBBING* IT IN.

MAYBE IF WE THREATEN TO GO TO THE PRESS AND *SMEAR* THEIR GOOD NAME, WE COULD SQUEEZE THEM FOR SOME MORE *SCRATCH!*

CAN WE GO BACK TO CLOCK PUNS? THIS *RASH* OF OINTMENT JOKES IS ALL *DRIED UP.*

Suddenly a green light filled the cabin, and a weird moan echoed through the room.

I shushed everyone and said, "Did you guys hear that?"

"Wh-wh-wh-what was it?" Hockney trembled.

Pepe clutched his belly. "It was probably just my stomach, okay. Tonight, I had a second jar of pickle juice. I figure we were celebrating, so why not, okay?"

"Shh!" I said. "I heard something outside the window."

There was a moaning and scratching noise right on the other side of the cabin wall.

Rizzo stepped up and bravely shouted, "Okay, Beebus! We know that's you and one of your practical jokes! Cut it out!"

But then a voice came from behind us.

"I'm right here!" said Beebus. He was shivering in the corner with a blanket pulled up to his chin. "I won't pull any more jokes. Kermit's already being cool enough, not reporting me to the cops after what I did. I'm a changed thug."

"But if it's not Beebus..." Rizzo shivered. "Then it must be..."

We all slowly glanced over at the window, terrified.

"It's Big Chicken!" yelled Gonzo. "At long last!"

Hockney fainted, and Pepe started to hyperventilate.

"What do we do, yo?" Kip whimpered.

"Just relax," I whispered. "I have a plan. On the count of three, everyone follow my lead. One... two...three, ruuuuuun!"

It felt so good to be back in my own bed, even if it was directly above Chloe's. It took Curtis all of five seconds to curl up on my pillow and start some serious snoring.

I wasn't far behind him. My eyelids felt like they weighed a ton, and my brain started giving way to loopy dreams of riverboats and dog woods and wakeboarding...

HEY! FLIP-TOP! ARE YOU AWAKE?

"I am now!" I moaned. "Haven't we had enough human interaction for this week? Go to bed."

For once in her life, Chloe looked a little sad. "I've got something to say, big brother, and it's going to be very difficult for me...."

"I know," I grumped. "You want to thank me for saving you from the animatronic insects. It's okay.

I know that, despite our differences, you really love me and—"

"Oh, please!" Chloe squirmed. "I would never say any of that stuff. Ick!"

I was confused. "Really? Well, what is it you wanna tell me?"

Chloe tried to get it out. "I wanna say…I…I…"

Suddenly, Mom opened the door with the phone in her hand. "Danvers! You have a phone call. It's that Honeymelon guy. I told him it was past your bedtime, but he says it's an emergency."

Dr. Honeydew? At this hour? I grabbed the phone and said, "Hello?"

"My Muppetmorphosis?" I said. "Can't it wait until tomorrow? I'm beat."

"I'm afraid not!" Dr. Honeydew continued. "We've discovered a mysterious green light shining from an unspeakably powerful source of matter-altering energy. A nexus of confounding swirls of antimatter and portentous glowing vapors accompanied by an unidentified electromagnetic pulse emanating from the deepest, darkest recesses of…*outer space!*"

"Outer space?"

WAIT A MINUTE, OKAY! THE LITTLE GIRL WAS JUST ABOUT TO SAY SOMETHING, OKAY. YOU CAN'T JUST LEAVE US HANGING ON LIKE THAT! IT IS CRUELTY, OKAY!

CHILL OUT, DUDE. IT'S CALLED A CLIFF-HANGER. JUST LIKE HOW DR. HONEYDEW MENTIONED OUTER SPACE—HEY, WAIT A MINUTE! YOU CAN'T JUST MENTION OUTER SPACE AND THEN END THE BOOK LIKE THAT! A DOUBLE CLIFF-HANGER IS TOTALLY UNCOOL!

CATCH UP ON DANVERS'S FIRST TWO ADVENTURES!

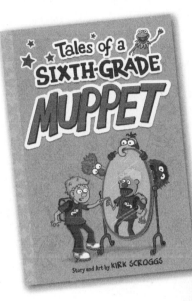

Representative **KIRK SCROGGS** started as an intern fresh out of college, first wrangling chickens for The Great Gonzo, then working his way up to junior fishmonger for council member Lew Zealand. After a brief stint with Rowlf the Dog, where his focus was leash law and barking permits, Scroggs felt muzzled and grew tired of dog-eat-dog local politics. Then he met Sam Eagle, and his career soared as he took to the national stage, writing wholesome, patriotic, all-American manifestos like *Our Nation's Youth: Boy, Are We in Trouble!* and the influential *Wiley and Grampa's Creature Features: Monster Fish Frenzy*.